Modernizing
The Betty:
Part 1

MeiMei Long

DEDICATION

Mom and
To all the Bettys at heart

Contents

ACKNOWLEDGMENTS

The founders of the Betty Neels fansite, The Uncrushable Jersey Dress, and the FaceBook group, and the encouraging members who encourage my writing – Dank U Wel!

1. Sun & Candlelight... Refracted

I disliked the twins and Nanny in Sun and Candlelight and wanted them gone from Alethea's life. A fresh start... how to create that happier future for her and Sarre was the priority in my mind.

Sun & Candlelight... Refracted, Part 1

Updating Betty Neels's Sun & Candlelight

*** Gentle Reader, In a bit of 'Sliding Doors', I start off near the end of Sun & Candlelight... please be patient as you wade through this first foray into RDD and all Neels/ Dutch... Hope this elicits kind emotions, dank u wel ***

Sun & Candlelight... Refracted (Part 1)

Alethea van Diederijk was arranging the flowers she had picked when the household's general factotum, Al, a middle-aged Cockney, came to her with a message from her husband, Sarre, the renown orthopedic surgeon. to say that he wouldn't be able to get home to lunch after all, that Al would take her to the airport in his stead, and that he hoped she would have a good holiday.

Alethea stood with the scissors in her hand, staring at him. "But he can't! ' she cried. "Al, are you sure that's what he said? ' Al nodded. "Ho, yus, ma'am. ' He eyed her knowingly. "It ain't ter your liking, neither, eh? '

She put the scissors down carefully, rammed the flowers in an untidy bunch into a priceless Sevres vase and took off her gardening gloves. "No, Al, it isn't quite. . . I'm a bit disappointed. ' She turned her back to pick up a dropped flower and when he asked if she would have her lunch on a tray in the sitting room she said yes, that would do, thank you, and waited until he had gone before she turned round.

She was so unhappy that she was past tears. Sarre could have telephoned, not sent that cold, polite message. He hadn't wanted the embarrassment of saying goodbye, she supposed, or to give her the chance of talking to him. She looked at her bruised arms and wondered how he could have been so gentle with her when he treated them, if he was so utterly indifferent to her. He was a kind man; perhaps he thought it kinder to let her go without seeing her again.

She wandered out into the garden again. What had she said or done in the last few days to make him so determined to send her away? She had thought he would have been pleased to see how happy his 11-year old twins were with her; she had never said a word to him about them and Nanny actively sabotaging her entrée into married life, but he must have noticed how both young Sarel and Jacomina had changed towards her.

She wasn't going to be able to bear it any longer. Half way up the staircase she stopped to look up at one of Sarre's ancestors, a handsome man who must have had the girls eating out of his hand.

"I shan't come back," she told him. And she meant it.

She made a pretence of eating the lunch Al served so carefully and then because it was time to go, she went upstairs to put on the jacket of her new outfit, a charming skirt and blouse in honey-coloured crepe-de-chine not in the least suitable for travelling. She had changed it at the last moment, because she had made up her mind to see Sarre before she caught the train and she wanted to look her best. She went to the dining room next and poured herself a glass of brandy; she loathed the stuff, but she needed something to make her brave enough to tell him that she wasn't coming back, and more than that, that she loved him and that was why.

She felt a little peculiar as she got into the car. Everyone had crowded into the hall to say goodbye and hope that she would be back soon, and she had time to beg Nanny – her nemesis-and-now-wannabe-friends-because-Old-Nanny-does-not-want-to-lose-her-cushy-job – to look after the children and to tell Mrs McCrea to make an extra large cake for the weekend. And once in the car, beside Al, she told him to go to the clinic first. "I'll be very quick, only a few minutes," she explained. "There's something I want to tell. That is. . '

"Cor, lummy, ma'am, your don't 'ave to explain, I ain't that feeble in the 'ead. The guv ain't 'alf lucky, 'having your ter love 'im. '

Which left her speechless.

The forecourt of the clinic was crowded. Alethea asked Al to let her out at the entrance before finding a parking space and hurried in through the swing doors. The outpatients' department was full but not as full as all that. Surely Sarre would be able to spare her a few minutes; besides. Doctor Jaldert was there too.

She crossed the tiled floor to the desk. The nurse on duty there was a stranger to her and when she asked to see Sarre she was told

3

politely that no, that wasn't possible, not for at least an hour or more. "But I'm his wife," explained Alethea. "T know he'll see me besides, there aren't very many patients. ' "I'm sorry, Mevrouw van Diederijk, it isn't possible it has nothing to do with the patients. '

Surely Sarre hadn't given instructions that he didn't want to see her? But he didn't know that she would be coming. . . Alethea fought an urge to burst into tears. "Would you let him know I'm here? ' And if she had to go on much longer, she thought wearily, she would run out of her meagre, quite dreadful Dutch. The nurse answered her with stony politeness. "That is also not possible, mevrouw."

Something went pop inside Alethea's unhappy head. She got up from the seat the nurse had begged her to take and before that astonished young woman could do anything about it, had marched to the nearest door and opened it. What was more, she told herself as she did so, she would open every door in the place until she found him. That her recklessness was due to the brandy she had drunk before she left the house to give her courage she chose to ignore. She had the first door open before the nurse reached her. She was aware of her urgent voice in her ear but she didn't listen.

The first room was empty.

The second room contained a meeting in full progress, a group of distinguished men and women. Among them, Anna.

The stony-faced nurse placed her hand on Alethea's forearm, "I am sorry, Mevrouw van Diederijk, but I must direct you to the public area."

Alethea stood tall, looked sharply at the hand, which was flushingly dropped as the nurse remembered her place. It would not do to manhandle the wife of the hospital's most distinguished

4

surgeons. Especially in a meeting room full of medical staff who were looking agog.

"I shall find my own way out, nurse," Alethea murmured. To Anna, a curt nod, urged on by the brandy, "Please tell my husband that I came to kiss him good-bye," and with a graceful turn of the heel, she strolled through the hospital back to the car.

Al was deeply engrossed in the Daily Mirror's breathless coverage of a magnificent scrum during the latest round of the Webb Ellis rugby when Alethea approached. He sprang up from behind the steering wheel to open the door and saw her seated. She sat bolt upright all the way to the train station, lost in thought.
"I tried to talk to him. How could he air out our dirty laundry at the hospital? Now they all know. He said he wanted me to go. Living with me – he is miserable. As much as I love him, he is right, I am not happy."

Alethea thought, "I guess I am not fated for doctors. First, Nick chucks me for nurse Marie. Now, Sarre has chosen Doctor Anna…"

The drive past the university and Groningen train station to the airport was scenic even in the cold weather.
At the airport, Al saw her through security to the VIP lounge, and filled her in on the arrangements to Grandma Thomas's home. Sarre had arranged for Alethea to be met at the airport and driven to Little Braugh.

After she gave impulsive hug to this kind man who brought rainbows into the Groningen house, Al handed her a bulky envelope with her name on it, in Sarre's frightful penmanship. In the envelope were a myriad of papers, including instructions on her bank accounts, credit cards, bank access cards, and a new mobile phone. Her allowance would now be paid monthly into the accounts – a sum that made her eyes water. She was to find a suitable house that would be put in her name, as had been explained at the solicitor's office so many weeks ago, make use of his cottage in the Lake District, as well as the Colt Sapporo. Which would arrive at Grandma's in a fortnight. He thought of everything, Alethea mused, absentmindedly extracting the VISA, Mastercard, and American Express Black card from their sleeves. With a flourish, it concluded with "All the best on a safe journey and all my love to Grandmother Thomas and Mrs Bustle."

How ironic, thought Alethea, "Everyone gets his love but me."

The public announcement speaker interrupted her melancholy, "Ladies and gentlemen, the flight to London has been postponed 3 hours due to late arrival of airport."

When others muttered and scrambled to their cell phones, Alethea belatedly realised she would not be arriving at Little Branaugh til late. It would be better for all if she stayed in London and then make her way to Granny's. Her arms still sore from the rescue, Alethea gingerly eased herself down at a telephone in the VIP lounge, and dialed granny.

Grandmother Thomas, called to the phone by Mrs Bustle, was matter-of-fact, "My dear, I can hear your achy muscles. After that terrible ordeal, I want you to rest, not rushing about."

Tears not to far in her voice, Alethea sniffed, "I am trying as best I can, Granny, but the plane…"

"Oh, I don't mean that, child, I say Praise the Lord for the delay. Once you land, you stay in a nice hotel and sleep around the clock for a few days. How good of Sarre to give you those credit cards, he knows I would not like you take up the first budget hostel, and knowing you, that might happen."

"Granny, I promise you that I will not do that. I will book right now and call you with the details."

Alethea hung up and looked at her mobile phone, which was the latest model with her contact information, Cloud storage subscription, and a credit card preloaded. Surfing to the App Store, it took only a few minutes to download hotel and travel applications and locate a selection of hotels. The Goring was rejected out of hand – Alethea wanted discretion – and found just the place offered at a steep discount for late bookings like herself. She even got an upgrade to a two-bedroom suite with a kitchen, living room, and a small dining room.

An idea came to mind, she could have Philly and Patty over, might as well fill up the place and give benefit of Sarre's largesse to her hardworking friends. it was high time to reconnect with her friends and offer them a night out. A jolly girls catch-up. A swift call to the girls was met with pleasing reception, they would pack to join her on night #2.

Finding some comfort in that, Alethea then contacted the shuttle service Al had booked to postpone her arrangements to a later date later in the week, at present unknown. Lastly, it was to hear granny's voice approving her plans. The smiling young man, who could not help but admire this poised young woman among the grumpy business people taking the flight delay personally, was more than obliging to help her print her hotel reservation at the computers in the business centre.

With two hours to go, Alethea gave herself a shake – and reached into her handbag to find pen and paper and wrote out everything she would tell Grandmother Thomas later.

"Darling Grandmother, Remember your words when I confided in you Sarre's proposal? You said, 'Companionship in marriage is important, you know, so is mutual respect and liking. It is possible to love someone without any of these things, even to dislike them.' How funny you emphasized 'companionship'. That is the same word that Sarre employed in his proposal 'I shall enjoy your companionship and be proud to have you at my table.'

Unfortunately, Grandmother, Sarre no longer wants my companionship, and has arranged for me to return to England. There is someone else, a surgeon colleague of his who he has known for yonks and yonks. He has had her at our gatherings when I presided over our table as the lady of the house, and I can only say that they suit each other. He speaks hours to her whereas he avoids talking to me.

There is a song, Sometimes Love Just Ain't Enough, and my feelings for my husband counted as little against his feelings for her. Although I am quite saddened to say good-bye to my life in Holland and my beloved Dutchman, I want you to know that he is behaving decently by providing me a monthly allowance. That he respects me enough to do that will surely ease my heartmending. There is no need to return to nursing. I have the use of his cottage in the country but for now, I want to come home to you, dear Granny."

Sun & Candlelight… Refracted, Part 2

Updating Betty Neels's Sun & Candlelight

Professor Sarre van Diederijk came back to a home empty of his beloved wife, Alethea. He deliberately stayed away until Al passed on word that he had personally seen her comfortably to the airport. Weary not just physically, he quietly opened the door, longing for his bed. It had been a trying week with his orthopaedic patients, and the children staging their disappearance and Alethea almost losing her life in searching for them.

The night he rescued them all made him realize too late the personal cost of his reticence to be firm with the children and Nanny. In the end, the children changed their minds about Alethea and even Nanny decided to accept his second wife's role as lady of the house and they all fell over themselves to show her their respect. But for months Alethea had to endure – alone in a new country not knowing the language – unnecessary strife to win their acceptance – continuous disrespect, a white rat planted in her bed, smashing of his gift of the music box, hourly slights, continual cold-shouldering.

Sure, she put a brave face through it all. He smiled wryly, recalling how Alethea's dear face lit up the morning the children and Nanny accepted her. But then, why would she not? For the time being, she was probably relieved not have to put up a front in her own home. "The Mrs is safely away, guvn'r, everything set for her."

Lost in thought at the threshold of his study, Sarre turned to Al, "I could not have trusted her care to a better set of hands, old friend."

"She was ever so sad to not see you at the hospital, guv. Wandered around the place for almost half an hour." Al's lower lip steadfastly refused to give into his emotions, the effect of which it gave it all away.

"It could not be helped, you see," replied Sarre smoothly, putting his briefcase down on his desk.

Al eyed the master of the house, his head cocked to one side, "Yes, I do see, guv." Turning to leave, Al switched back to detachment, "Mrs McCrea has supper ready in half an hour."

Sinking down into the armchair in his study, Sarre rubbed his eyes. It was right to send Alethea back to her Grandmother's home. While her triumph in Groningen was fresh. It was better this way. Better she leaves Holland thinking well of the place. Better than again watching another woman's smiles slowly changing into pursed contempt – he could not bear to see that happen again.
***

"But when exactly will Alethea, I mean Mama, be back home?" asked Jacomina for the fourth time, morosely sulking into her dessert, a whipped-cream topped gateau aux noisettes.

Seated at the head of the splendid dining table, seemingly placid, Sarre resolved to put his household to rights. The children were his, but children no longer. At age eleven, the twins both needed to be ready to take their place in the world. They had to act better in company.

"Lieverd, is this how a young lady of 11 acts at the table?" Sarre inquired mildly.

Jacomina's eyes widened into circles. Her brother Sarel lowered his – this was a side of their father they rarely saw, or wanted to see, and for good reason.

Nanny's eyes narrowed, "Mijnheer, the little miss cannot be faulted for lack of practice…"

Sarre raised his eyebrows and leveled Nanny with a cool stare, "Quite right, Nanny, I take you at your word. From now on, they shall spend time downstairs. They are becoming young adults and as such, they have outgrown the playroom. There is that morning room they can study in, much more convenient to the library."

Nanny turned purple, aware that the ground was shifting under her feet faster than the old cottage a week ago. "This is Mevrouw's idea – she wants shod of me. I remember when she…"

"Nanny, you forget yourself…" warned Sarre.

Sarrel burst in, attempting to diffuse the scene, "What a good idea, Father, we are getting too tall for the chairs and tables in the playroom…"

"Since you will not be growing shorter, son, you can start tomorrow. Al will be in charge of helping you move," murmured Sarre.

Not one bit deterred by his son's intervention, the Professor made clear to everyone who was head of the family, "Dear Nanny, you can be excused for the evening from now on. The children are old enough to do their schoolwork in the morning room, say their prayers and ready themselves for bed, bath and beyond. You have worked too many days of long hours. And I have lost track of time, I beg your forgiveness. Now you deserve more time to yourself."

Standing up, Sarre swept up the children in the direction of his study, pausing to deliver more news of change, "Our cousin Juppe's daughter will now be in charge of the children in the evenings. She has been accepted into a place at the University and will be staying with us starting in a week."

"Oh, cousin Annemieke?" cried Jacomina, "She is superb, almost as wonderful as Mama."

Sarre closed his eyes momentarily, "Yes, almost as wonderful as my Alethea."

Sun & Candlelight… Refracted, part 3

Updating Betty Neels's Sun & Candlelight

"I wonder if he is smiling at Anna, laughing with Anna," thought Alethea, sinking into the armchair at the crowded VIP lounge at the airport, coping with a further delay with the remnants of a chicken pot pie and a glass of Cabernet Sauvignon perched on her knee. "Oh, I must stop this, mooning over this man. Of course he is with her, it was Sarre who brought another person into this marriage."

Renewed anger at being called 'plump' by Anna, and Sarre grinning at the creature's wit, Alethea jolted her arm, knocking down her handbag. And her new mobile phone fell out, with a crunch of glass as the screen shattered.

She burst into tears.

The young attendant, who gave his name as Floris, hurried over from across the room with a box of tissues, "Now there, Ma'am, what can I do?"

At her shaky pointed finger, Floris quickly assessed the situation. "Let me gather up that purse of yours and the nice mobile phone…"

"Oh, I am so sorry to cause housekeeping more work…" she hiccupped, conscientious of the stares of a middle-aged business woman holding a Birkin bag and several pompous looking men.

"Oh, Ma'am, the screen has just shattered in a spider pattern but it has a protective layer so there is absolutely no harm done."

"I am normally not so clumsy…"

"These new phones travel everywhere, yes, even the floor sometimes. If you have the Apple Care Plus plan, they can replace it for you in London." With a glance at her person, noting the shoes, the scarf, the hat, and the handbag, Floris continued, "I would be almost certain, Mevrouw van Diederijk, that you are covered. Would you like me to help you check through the computers here?"

Looking mournfully at the mobile phone, still barely, with a kaleidoscope effect of dimmed light refracting through the shattered glass screen, Alethea looked up through the tissue, "Would you please? You are such a dear."

In the space of 20 minutes, with Floris leaning over Alethea at a computer workstation, they had contacted the care centre through the website and performed a diagnosis online. It was a friendly conversation with a friendly Irish call centre attendant. "Mrs van Diederijk, there is no problem at all getting you back on line with a nice replacement. A very modest fee, what could be better. London you say, we have retail stores where you just bring in your phone tomorrow and we can get you set up. I just booked you into a 12 noon Genius Bar appointment into our Regent Store location. May we also interest you in a good case against drops and water-damage?" Agreed, nothing could be better than that. The two were pleased with a job well done by all sides...

"Hey, boy! We need more ice here for the wine!"

Alethea looked up from her computer monitor to see a stocky man with beady eyes and a paunch, holding up an empty glass of wine by the rim, wagging it. Floris, flushed, attempted to excuse himself. But after days of stewing about Anna's unflattering remarks, Alethea decided to let loose some choice retorts.

Standing to her full height, she stared at the man, "Sir, I think you did not see there is another station there amply supplied with ice. And I should be kind enough to let you know that over on this side of the pond, we call employees 'sir'. Nor do we ever put ice in our wine."

***

Around 8 pm, Alethea was giving Floris a wide smile of gratitude as he escorted her and her carryon luggage to the gate. "Dank u wel, Mr Floris, I don't know what I would have done without you.

13

I am feeling so much better, you do not need to roll my bag to plane."

He had to, thought Floris. True there was no rush to pick up some documentation at a gate three over from the plane to London, but he could not let his shift finish without one more smile from this delightful lady. Such a change from hard-as-nails business types.

As he handed over her bag while she prepared to go down the gangway, Floris bade her a smooth flight. She looked at him with a grin, "I hope no more ill-humoured men from Toronto come into your lounge tonight."

"He definitely was not a Torontonian. As you shall see, we Dutch have a very special relationship with Canadians."

Floris bent over and kissed her hand, "Tot ziens, Mevrow van Diederijk, what a warrior queen you are, the Professor is indeed a lucky man."

She squeezed his heart with another magnificent smile and turned herself towards England. Floris watched her splendid walk, enjoying the view, then was interrupted by a well-dressed elderly gentleman.

"Young man, did you say, 'Mevrow van Diederijk'?"

Shaking off his reverie, Floris answered, "Yes, sir, that was she."

"Ach, talk about ships in the night, we just landed and missed my new daughter-in-law."

***

"Sarre, are you listening to me?" Anna snapped her fingers at the Professor gazing out the window of the consultants meeting room at the trees budding in the midsummer morning.

He turned suavely as the meeting finishing up. "But of course." He made a valiant effort to disguise his inner thoughts. Alethea, so well-mannered, was not answering her mobile phone, must have seen his name on Call Display.

It was a surprise when his Father stopped by enroute to his own home, Al patiently waiting in the car. His father was all compliments on Alethea, relaying some of his conversation with the young man. Another fellow who has fallen under her spell, thought Sarre, gritting his teeth. Sighing, that is what happens when you fall in love with a beautiful woman, Sarre smiled wryly.

Anna heaved her patient notes into her Kelly bag, "I was saying yes to drinks tonight. How fortunate that your father's flight itinerary advanced almost a month. We must toast to the van Diederijk being reunited again. What time is Alethea opening the doors?"

Pocketing his fountain pen, Sarre absentmindedly answered, "I think 7 PM, Alethea is not there. She has gone to her Grandmother's."

Mildly surprised, Anna inquired, "That English lady, but she was just here. And now Alethea is off visiting her…"

Looking around the other medical doctors in the room, Anna quirked a brow, "And she came into this very room yesterday telling me that she came to 'kiss you good-bye'. Careful, Sarre, 'visiting granny' just screams 'the honeymoon is over'.. Two times unlucky at the altar, old friend, maybe you should consult our marriage and family therapy team…"

Everyone in the room was affronted by Anna's words.

Very mildly, too mildly, Sarre turned cold eyes at Anna, "I beg your pardon?"

Anna caught herself, taken aback by the look of distaste on his face, aware she has crossed a line, "My apologies, Sarre, this was tactless of me."

Looking down at Anna from across the room, Sarre smoothly delivered a reposte, "This is getting to be a habit, Anna, you were most tactless to call my beloved wife 'plump' in her own home. Being the gracious hostess and kind lady that she is, you were not called onto the carpet. But be rest assured, I remember that."

Flushed and perspiring, Anna looked shamefacedly at the Professor, "I have apologize to you, Sarre, and to Alethea, it will not happen again."

"See that it does not."

***

Part 4

"This won't happen again, will it?" said Alethea to the Genius Bar staffer, "This one dare not fall apart in its drop-resistant and water-proof case."

"There is no reason, Ma'am, in this whole wide world," the young man stammered, as Alethea beamed happily at him.

"And why they call you 'geeks', I will never understand. You made this all so simple to understand and use."

He gulped, "I have no idea at all. Now, the last step is to turn on and wait how many voice mails and messages you missed. I should warn you, it could take a while to populate. It depends on how popular you are." He grinned at his terrible pun.

"I just received this yesterday, so I won't be taking up more of your time."

"Ma'am, it is my pleasure to serve you. What are your plans for the rest of the day?" The young man continued his configuration.

"A spiritual afternoon before meeting my friends at Theobald's. A concert at St Martin in the Fields and a service at Holy Trinity Brompton – sermons in English!"
"You are quite an angel, so patient, if you don't mind my saying so," his ears turning bright red, "Ah, your phone is pinging, I am not surprised that you are more in-demand than you believe. Most of them came from a store named 'Sarre'…"

Alethea looked over his shoulder, "Oh! That is my husband's name."

"Anyone ever tell you he is a lucky man?"

***

In the middle of his afternoon rounds, Sarre felt his mobile phone vibrate. Nanny complaining about Al again? Al had his every confidence, he knew by the tea time, the children would be downstairs and the playroom a memory. His lips twitching at the thought, Sarre bent over another patient who was mending nicely.

17

Later on, he checked and saw a missed call from Alethea. It went to voice mail, a deliberately calm perfunctory message thanking him for the arrangements and yes, she would look for a house. Sarre saved this message, her voice was pleasing to him. Perhaps he had been too hasty to avoid her – he would have enjoyed a kiss from her, the first time she initiated anything beyond their carefully-negotiated parameters. Maybe he should have allowed more of that.

Sarre returned her call, which went to voice mail.

Alethea, as a lady, had turned off her cellphone during the concert.

***

Alethea stepped in Theobald's with pent up emotion and resolute. The lady minister had listened – an annulment was an option that was available to her, and much quicker way to set her to rights. She also felt more confident with different ways to proceed on a professional matter as well. Head held high, Alethea gave a silent prayer for the lesson of her interaction with Floris. Bullies cow people into silence and inaction – and Nick must not be allowed to continue his reign among the female staff at any hospital. She pursed her lips – if Matilde Solis, the former duchess of Huescar can go public, then the current wife of prominent orthopaedic surgeon can do the same.

She made her way to the human resources department.

****

"Alethea? What a surprise, come in," waved the affable personnel manager.

After a ten-minute wait, Alethea found herself seated and apprehensive in the plain office overlooking a hospital dumpster. "I believe you are wondering why I am here…" She began.

"No mystery at all, why skirt around the issue? We have your final cheque right here," Mrs Patel fumbled around in a cabinet, extracting Alethea's file, "ah, here it is. Oh, and yes, this…" She said with a grimace.

Handing over an envelope that seemed to contain a nasty bacteria, Mrs Patel continued, "Everyone gets one of these."

Skimming the page, Alethea raised her eyebrows, "Nick Penrose wrote personally to everyone here at Theobald's?"

"I imagine his lawyer did. We helped, of course, the phrasing had to be right."

"The undersigned, Nick Penrose… I acknowledge my series of unacceptable aggressive behaviour towards has done a discredit to the medical profession… And apologize profusely… Furthermore, I accept the sanctions and conditions of continued practice… ."

Skipping ahead…"Restrictions on communicating with all female staff ie to never be alone, any and all personal relationships with female staff are banned, oh it covers training on communication with male and female staff and patients, from alpha to omega…" A satisfied look came over Mrs Patel's face.

"How did this come to be?"

"Nick Penrose thought Miss Emma Chow in cardiology would be complacent. And she was, i think kickboxing is the gentlest tool in her arsenal."

Alethea felt lightheaded, "Kickboxing?"

"I understand men's surgical found it all to their liking, David versus Goliath. Quite a list of people who came forward as witnesses including some on your old orthopaedic ward, Miss Chambers, who documented his disgraceful actions… Nick Penrose is more sorry than you will ever know and I want to give everyone, you included, our apologies for his making our hospital a toxic environment. Be assured everyone is actively monitoring. We shall not tolerate harassment any longer."
****

Part 5 Sun & Candlelight, Refracted
***notice that i have used some of TGB's phrases here

"He just simply wanted to get away, did you see the fear in his eyes?" snorted Sue, watching Nick Penrose scurry away.

Just two minutes previous, Alethea and an obliging cab driver met Patty, Philly, and Sue who were finishing their shift at Theobald's when Nick Penrose was strolling by the hospital side entrance. He took one look at the four ladies, conscious of the censorious gazes tracking his actions, "Oh, umm, Alethea, I mean Mrs van Diederijk, how good you look. I mean, I have to, er, I want to offer my apologies for my unacceptable behaviour."

Giving him a level glance, Alethea gave a cool response, "It is good that you have learnt your lesson, Nick." For good measure, "Everyone at Theobald's is here to help you mend your ways."

"Er, yes, I must be off, ladies," Nick nervously rushed off, much to the humor of the four nursing chums.

"So should we, the cases are in the boot," intoned the grinning cab driver, with a flourish opening doors, "Your destination is…"

"...Ladies Nights!" they chorused, as the taxi merged into light traffic.

****

"But my dear, how can you be absolutely sure?" Mrs Thomas asked.

Alethea sat down in maillot bathing suit and robe, speaking to her grandmother with the speaker function of her mobile phone. "He is always speaking with her, and invites her home and spends all hours with Anna..."

"To which I say, Tut tut, men can be unthinking. These alone do not constitute infidelity nor sufficient grounds to end your marriage. You now must simply ask Sarre if he is in love with this Anna. And observe him when he answers."

The front door to the suite opened, with Sue, Patty, and Philly tiptoeing in from their dip in the hotel pool.

"Yes, Granny, but he does not want to talk... and I have tried."

Alethea could almost see Granny's brows rise, "Simply ask him, straightforward question, child."

"You are right, of course, Granny. Please enjoy your supper," as their call ended.

A glass of wine appeared in Alethea's peripheral vision, held by its stem by Philly. Philly who had suggested the cab make a stop to fill up the hotel fridge with groceries including eggs, sausage, frozen pizza, crisps, shortbread, Earl Grey sachets, and most important of all, Waitrose wine. 'Our personal project to Reintegrate Alethea into the world of British cuisine.'

Sue sympathetically, "Sorry, ducks, your Grandmother says that …"

"That she agrees with you lot, I need to hear Sarre and most of all see Sarre when I ask him. I cannot do this by phone."

Head in her hands, Alethea sniffed, "But this is impossible. And going back to Holland would be fruitless. I even went to the hospital to find him and he would not see me."

Patty held up the mobile phone, "I think it is significant that there were missed calls from him. I am sure you can talk to him without chasing him all over the Netherlands…"

Sue slapped her forehead, "Oh my stars, we forgot, you can call him and speak with him and see him on your mobile using FaceTime!"

"Lets do this now! It is 5:30 pm here, what time is it in Groningen…?"
***

Sarre looked at the antique grandfather clock in the master bedroom – he had half an hour before the 7 PM drinks downstairs. An outpatients clinic that ran over, a drive back home that took longer than usual, barely enough time to ready himself to be the gracious host. Running a comb through his damp hair, Sarre absentmindedly saw his mobile phone light up. Caller Display: Alethea…

Swiftly picking up and engaging the connection, the screen showed a live video of a torso, a comely torso clad in a mauve-coloured maillot, hesitantly, her soft voice, "Sarre…"

"My dear, it is I, can you tilt your screen, as I can see only your bosom…"

22

"Yes, I have it leaning against a vase on the table and need a book to keep it steady. Ah, that is how it works . Is it better now?" Aletha asked.

Sarre stood there drinking in her exquisite face. Of course he felt better admiring her.

Clearing his throat, Sarre spoke, "Just so, Alethea. Please excuse my dishabille, I have just stepped out of the shower."

Although there was so much of Sarre on view than she had ever laid eyes on, with a strategically placed towel, her chums craning their necks discreetly to check out the view from across the room, Alethea plunged on, "Sarre, I have a very important question to ask you and I very much need you to give an unequivocable answer. I would seek an annulment and release you if you are in love with Anna or anyone. Are you in love…"

Sarre looked intently into her eyes "Alethea, four days after we met, you have grasped my heart and still hold it in your hands. Remember when I hauled you out of that cellar, I said by sun and candlelight…"

Alethea said, "Yes, you said by sun and candlelight, it's Elizabeth Barret Browning, isn't it. 'I love thee to the level of each days most quiet need, by sun and candlelight." Do you really, Sarre, You're in love with me, it's so silly of me, i've fallen in love with you. You'll find it hard to believe after Nick… but of course i've never been in love before only thought I had – it's quite different."

Sarre spoke very quietly, "Yes, it is, isn't it? I have found myself in love a dozen times, and that includes my first wife but when I fell in love with you, I knew that none of them counted – only you, my darling… I want you for my wife."

Alethea had tears in her eyes and snuffled into a hanky, her chums in the background wiping their eyes.

With regret in his voice, Sarre continued, "It hasn't been all roses for you, has it. The children, oh, don't look so surprised, I have eyes in my head and my hearing is excellent – besides they came and told me all about it… And Nanny, at the beginning she was eaten up with jealousy…"

"What?" interjected Alethea, interrupting Sarre, "What are you saying, that you knew what was going on, while it was going on…"

Sarre admitted it, "I saw the water stain in the playroom when I said good night to the children and guessed that this was the source of your dress water spot…"

As calmly as she could, Alethea inquired, "And how did you discipline Sarel for throwing the vase and flowers at my gown?"

"I waited to see how things would unfold," replied Sarre, smoothly.

"And Jacomina and Sarel for stomping on my music box, tell me what you said to them."

"I said I was angry but not at them."

Alethea was on a roll: "And Nanny, you knew that Nanny was jealous, you did not stop her from defying my role as your childrenès stepmother, from encouraging them to sneer at me, to speak disrespectfully in Dutch to me, to be bloody rude to me for days and weeks on end. Do you have any idea what it is like to not know what I would find in my bed every night after I found that rat Caesar underneath the covers. And to be unable to feel peace and comfort in my own home because the knives could be anywhere. A

Nanny suffering from paranoia and dementia. And then smug Anna…!"

Sarre spoke up, "About Anna, I have been at fault there. I wanted to tease you to arouse your interest, to make you jealous…"

Alethea was taken aback, "Sarre, I would not have thought you would be capable to doing something so puerile. You knew how distressed I was that Nick replaced me with that nurse, and yet you copied the same thing, throwing another woman in my face, in my own home. Oh, what a contemptuous thing to do."

With fire in her eyes, Alethea started raising her voice," I am realizing now how right your statement was, that I am good for the children, but Sarre, **you did nothing to make sure they are good to me** and **good for me**!"

"You feel love for me, but for me, love is also an action, and you just stood back and watch me try to work with antagonists in a war zone."

"You avoided me, talked in coded language that implies nothing, do not talk to me, brings home a woman who called me FAT in my own drinks party. You call that 'love, cherish, and respect'? I refuse to share my future with someone who professes to love me but won't even protect me in my own house."

Voice breaking into sobs, Alethea wiped her eyes, "Sarre, you wouldn't guess in a thousand years, I am not coming back."

PART 6 SUN & CANDLELIGHT, REFRACTED

Alethea step out of the taxi, having dropped off Philly, Patty, and Sue off at Theobald's. Three nights together – she in the master suite, Sue and Patty in the room with twin beds, and Philly on the pull-out sofa that everyone declared was the most comfortable bed in the whole place. The three chums filled in Alethea on their upcoming vacation in Canada – Montreal, Ottawa, Toronto. In the fridge were Sainsbury breakfasts, Marks & Spencers supper fare, the remnants of late night carryouts of all cuisines, and the most important occupant, wine from Waitrose. Muzzily, Alethea considered herself, thoroughly reintegrated into British cuisine!

Nodding at the reception desk, and ready to hop back into bed after their last night out, Alethea contemplated how simple it would be to pack her carryon. The bliss of having a washing machine in the suite, all her clothes were clean. A copy of Laugh Your Way to a Happy Marriage light and flat. The benefit of a fridge and friends who love to help one shop for Granny and Mrs Bustle, the hamper with special jams and sundries are all set to go. Two more nights, two more nights of video calls with Sarre, then the shuttle service would drop her off at Granny's.

That he had been taking steps on his own initiative to change things at the house – even before their first and very emotional video call – melted her. "Come back and Be my love…" he even wooed her with the Songs of Solomon. There were still some outstsnding issues to be resolved – Alethea was adamant about Nanny whereas Sarre was still unsure on how exactly to make it happen. As for the children, regardless of whether she returned or not, the twins had do something after school and on weekends outside of their privileged bubble, a charcter-building activity that Alethea insisted. She approved of Jacomina taking dressmaking lessons near the university and Sarel volunteering twice weekly at an animal shelter.

Still, there was no need to make hasty decisions, and she was prepared herself at least another month or into the fall. Alethea could only gently respond to Sarre's overtures that a new type of dynamic in Groningen – with a second home in Britain – was worth considering.

I could even show my face in London again, Alethea sighed with contentment in the elevator. Many opportunities when I decide to go back to work. I need to keep up my licence, even the rare, occasional parttime will do to keep the government regulators happy. And even at Theobalds … Nick Penrose is a chastened man, by personnel with a little help from my friends. She let slip a wicked grin at how the Sisterhood takes care of each other, a whisper, "Put the Blame on dames, Nick…"

Strolling down the corridor, Alethea hummed the famous Rita Hayworth song from the film 'Gilda'. Inserting her key into the lock, she entered the suite, tossed her hat onto the credenza, andremoved her leather gloves. "That's the story that went around, but here's the real low-down… Put the blame on Mame, boys, put the blame on Mame."

It was a triumphal feeling, as Alethea flung her cardigan over the armchair, the next she grabbed the clasp of Grandmother van Diederijk's necklace of Russian sapphires and diamonds… "One night she started to shim and shake… that brought on the Frisco quake… "Put the blame on Mame, boys, put the blame on Mame…"

Alethea caught her reflection in the mirror, a 27-year old God-fearing independent woman who can make her own way through life, vibrant, attractive, positive. Who commanded respect. From her professional peers. And would demand it from her home life regardless of whether she returns to Sarre or she proceeds with the annulment. If she married again, mutual respect, communication, and fidelity had at the core from the very beginning.

"Mame did a dance called the Hitchee-coo, that's the thing that looma grew…" Her wedding ring hit the table next. "Put the blame on Mame, boys, put the blame on Mame…"

Finally, Alethea did an elaborate curtesy to an imaginary audience of the Sisterhood and humming "Put the Blame on Mame" strutted down to her bedroom.
Smack into the solid wall of Sarre. In a towel.

He gave her a considered look, "Alethea, my darling, you asked me, 'Do you have any idea what it is like to not know what I would find in my bed every night?'. I am here to answer your very question… No, I have no idea. And from now on, neither will you."

He quirked an eyebrow at her, sweeping an arm to present himself, and asked, "Worth considering?"

As impulsively as her choice to accept this man's proposal, Alethea threw caution to the winds. The only thing that Alethea could utter as she reached for him were the words Gilda said in the movie.

"Sure, I'm decent."

Part 7. Sun & Candlelight, Refracted

"Mevrouw Ferrer to see you, Mijheer,"

At his receptionist's announcement, Sarre was finishing up notes in his consulting rooms. He glanced at the clock, mentally calculating the time difference and the hours til he would be on FaceTime with Alethea.

It definitely was not the same as having her in his arms, but it would do for the time being. Normally he preferred baroque music to popular songs but Sarre had to admit Weekend in New England encapsulated his state of mind as Alethea's husband. Three weeks ago, Al had driven Nanny to her new home in Maastricht , the playroom converted to a crafts studio, and soon everything else will be ready for Alethea.

Until then, it suited them both, rather it suited him, to know Alethea was with her Grandmother and her friends. She was coming to like their future together.

His thoughts shifted to their newfound togetherness the previous month, Alethea being roused from slumber by the gliding of diamonds and sapphires against bare skin as he desultorily fastened her necklace. And Sarre's voice in her ear, "Lieveling, we have two-and-a-half hours to check out."

Burying her face into the pillow, the response was a sleepy, "Check out is not until Saturday."

Amused, Sarre laconically agreed, "Today is Saturday."

"You are not serious... What happened to Friday?" Alethea then blushed, "Oh, I suppose we don't need to get into that..."

Sarre drove the Colt Sapporo to London Southend airport, where his besotted wife saw him off onto a flight to Groningen, and then she pointed the wheel in the direction of Grandmother Thomas's abode.

Late summer in Essex always brought a cornucopia of fresh vegetables and fruit in the garden. And jam making in the kitchen kept Alethea from getting too underfoot of Mrs Bustle. Walks daily to the quiet village church where she found solace in the ancient service, solitude
in arranging flowers, and security in the pews looking at nothing in particular. Perhaps the future... In the evenings, she would keep quiet company with Granny, conversations about not much. There was not much to say.

"You take after me, my dear, not one to dither. Calling Sarre with one question. He gave you a clear answer. And then he drove all the way from Holland to meet you in London. For a busy man to spend three days with you talking, no stopping at Theobald's, a credit to you both."

Alethea nodded, "Thank you, Granny."

Mrs Thomas reached over to pat her granddaughter's hand, "My child, please know that you will always have a home with me in the event that you decide for an annulment..."

In her own thoughts, Alethea, who was brought up to consider fibs a grave sin, answered, "It would have to be a divorce now..." She pulled herself up short, and coughed, looking down at a suddenly-intriguing moss rose bush.

"A pleasant turn of events," murmured Granny, wisely.

The mobile phone pinged every evening, signal of the daily
video call from Groningen. Or Vienna. Or Hamburg. From
wherever Sarre was consulting and operating. Alethea had also met
her father and mother-in-law through the medium of FaceTime, as
well as Sarre's grandfather, a stately gentleman graciously
welcoming her into the family. He spent much time with the twins,
who were bewildered by the sweet but apparently voracious
Neptune. How could this gentle baby cat be capable of
systematically decimating the rodent population of Huis van
Diederijk? Caesar was the first to meet death-by-kitten.

But that was a rare deviation from their regular pattern of
private tete-a-tete video, whereupon Alethea would retire with her
mobile phone under a tree in the garden. Or behind the closed door
of her bedroom.

This rhythm was scarcely interrupted by the non-stop flight to
Montreal.

***

Patty had called, wailing about her unfortunate aerial yoga
accident, meaning that the three chums could not travel on holiday
to Canada as planned. Would Alethea take her place on this
fortnight holiday that would end at an international nursing
conference? The members of the older generation of both Alethea
and Sarre were very much in support – Granny thought that it was
another God-given opportunity to spread her wings. Her
grandfather-in-law waxed enthusiastically about Canadian
troops liberating the Netherlands.

A sum of money went to Patty for Alethea to take over
her vacation bookings and so it was that Sue, Phily, and Alethea
found themselves at Heathrow stepping onto a jet bedecked in Air
Canada livery.

"Would someone kiss Mr Darling van Diederijk for upgrading us to this business class pod?" sleepily intoned Philly from the now-flatbed seat.

"That would not be me," responded Sue, settling into a National Film Board of Canada documentary. "I volunteer Alethea."

The lady being discussed drained an after-meal cup of tea, and turned on her side to sleep for a few hours, her mobile phone plugged in to recharge, the screen saver of which was a photo of herself and Sarre at London Southend airport.

Part 8. Sun & Candlelight, Refracted

"Tea time break," teased Sue as the three chums noticed the familiar ping of an incoming FaceTime video call as they finished breakfast at their hotel near the Ottawa museum for the daily morning call between Sarre and Alethea. "Patty and I try yet another kind of organic herbal tea and you two can catch up in private."

"I have the best friends in the world," smiled Alethea, as she sipped her tea, and the connection brought Sarre's visage into focus on her mobile screen.
"Goedemorgen, Lieverd," he intoned deeply.

As per usual, Alethea responded in Dutch, "Jij bent min allerliefste liefie…" inevitably looking self-consciously around hoping their endearments were not understood by others in the cafe.

Sarre put on a bland face as her voice calling him 'dearest sweet of all time' made its usual impact on him. It had not been his usual practice to be so open in his affections but it was an old habit that he derived much pleasure in modifying. Alethea's persistence in her Dutch all through these weeks since her departure from Groningen impressed him all the more.

"Sarre, what did you think of the photo of us in front of 'The Man with Two Hats'? The Netherlands is everywhere in this city, tulips from the Dutch Royal Family every year and the Karsh gardens…"

"There were other people in the photograph, my darling? I noticed only you. Speaking of notice, tomorrow you all pick up the rental car and drive towards Toronto for the conference, but mind you, on the other side of the road."

"Don't worry, the roads here are very accommodating. Almost all packed, we shall leave with all our smalls washed. Thank you so much for arranging for us to stay at this Les Suites hotel downtown. So convenient to all the museums and Parliament and Byward Market and beaver tails…"
"Beaver tails, what on earth are those?"

"We preferred the vegetarian version after our Cantonese supper last night, Lieverd," said Alethea teasingly, "We are staying tomorrow night in Durham Region and then drive into our hotel in Toronto in the afternoon… It is walking distance to the convention hotel."
"An estimable convention hotel which unfortunately has no suites. I know you like to make your own cups of tea…" Sarre paused significantly, bringing to mind the exact circumstances of his acquiring that insight.

Sparing her blushes, Sarre changed topics, "Darling, I have some good news to tell you about Sarrel and Jacomina. As you predicted, they are taking to cousin Annemieke like ducks to water, and take all their meals downstairs… They have no desire to keep in touch with Nanny either, now that she's shown her true colours. But enough of that, I gird my loins about another matter."

Alethea set down her teacup, all ears.

"The twins' mother has been here visiting, she wants them to spend vacations in South America and other short breaks time with herself and her husband when they are in Europe, and perhaps move over there for school."

Alethea gasped, "What made her reappear?"

"After all this time, they decided to run tests – she had undiagnosed post-partum depression, leading to her actions and the breakdown of our relationship. Fortunately her psychological issues are now controlled, and Vicente Ferrer is very supportive of his 5th wife. She was too young, barely out of her teens, when I married her, before she could spread her wings. We three talked together. Ferrar had settled a substantial amount of money on her, and she inherited two houses from her family, and Sarrel and Jacomina are her heirs to that. Any children we have and yourself, dear, will inherit everything from me. It took the lawyers late nights to make it legal and airtight but in the end all very equitable, in the end.

Sarre paused, "And we all met together with Sarrel and Jacomina. They spent time getting to know her, just returned from a weekend in Venice all of them. I have had them to myself for ten years, and they have looked into good day schools over there. Lieveling, know this, the twins are adjusting nicely to the Ferrers in their lives, you will be pleased to see that."

***

The next evening, the ladies tossed their bags onto the beds in the Holiday Express Clarington, in Bowmanville, giggling. "I say, Sue, a good thing we took the scenic drive on that number 115/35 road, no one around to see you veering off to their driving side of the road," laughed Alethea.

"We needed to pull into that Tim Hortons so I could steady my nerves!" Philly kicked off her shoes.

Lifting one eyebrow, Sue averred, "A double espresso does that? At least I got us to the. bake shop in Orono."

"Alethea, how did you ever learn to speak Dutch like that? You clever thing. The owners treated you like royalty. Dutch royalty!"

"Stuff and nonsense," murmured Alethea vaguely, as she configured her mobile phone for hotel wi-fi.

"Oh, it's time for the Daily van Diederijk photo upload, let's head to the swimming pool, Philly. Tomorrow after we turn in the rental car in Toronto, we can start on the Archibald's fruit wine in the hotel."

Supper was a delightful fusion-cuisine bistro tucked into a side street in downtown Bowmanville, Alethea wondered how Sarre had friends even in such a small town to reserve it for them. Bistro Chanterelle's proprietor, Mr Leung, had trained in the Peninsula Hotel in Hong Kong, and in turn his staff made the ladies feel welcome and relaxed.
"Tell me," asked Sue, "when we were circling looking for parking, we came across this funny-looking house. It is out of place among the Victorian houses here in Bowmanville."

"Ah, that is the Octagon House, it is older than Canada, built in 1862. Not open to the public – the lady writer who made this reservation for you – she's the owner."

"My husband did say they go way back," Alethea brightened up, "Let's visit this Octagon Houseand take a photo of us three in front of it…"

"… So Sarre can see us in front of different architecture," teased Philly,
"That means we would be grinning all over Toronto! There's that new-age City Hall, the arts school on stilts, and the Tower…"

Mrs van Diederijk gave her friend a mock punch in the arm.

***

Part 9 Sun & Candlelight, Refracted

It was an easy drive after service at the Dutch Reformed Churchacross from Bowmanville cemetery and the zoo to Toronto. They had had a delirious fortnight together travelling across the Ottawa River to Quebec, practising their French, and now it was time to transition back into their profession, at the huge convention of nurses from all over the world.

The friends easily checked in their hotel in downtown Toronto with bell service taking care of transporting their bags and the case of Archibald's wine to their suite in due course.
***

"Cor, Are those islands out there?" whistled Sue, peering out the windows across from the hotel elevator banks high above Canada's largest city.

Studiously, having well-researched Fodors, Frommers, and the Lonely Planet, Philly cited, "According to my research, these islands were originally connected to the mainland but a fierce storm last century…"

"Did we ask for an indepth commentary?" Alethea looked on in mock horror as the bellman pushed the trolley down the corridor.

"Oh, I finally got Sarre on video call…" It was a chuckling Mrs van Diederijk whose visage connected on FaceTime, "Dearest, we made it to Toronto, to this scrumptious suite hotel… Oh..!." she turned pink as Sarre's unclad torso came into view.

"Liebling, my excuses, I was about to step into the the bath when your call came through. Is the room suitable?" his calm voice offered.

Pleading, Alethea urged Sarre, "Fine, Lieverd, a most lovely place, We just arrived with the trolley, now do cover yourself or you will catch a cold."

The chums followed the bellman in, breathlessly but decorously checking out the kitchen area with wine glasses, stove top, fridge. In a closet was the apartment-sized washer-dryer. The ladies kept opening doors – one set of French doors led to the bedroom with two beds from the living room with a pullout couch, and finally a pocket door revealed the washroom with floor-to-glass windows, a large jacuzzi, and a towel-clad Sarre.

"I am about to test the waters…" Sarre, leaning against the marble vanity, vaguely waved in the direction of the jacuzzi. Looking solid, reassuring, loving to her eyes.

"Sarre, is this really you?" Alethea approached him, like he were a spectre, afraid he might disappear like Eurydice if she got too close.

"None other."

From the threshold, Philly and Sue observed with eyes like saucers. The bellman removed Alethea's bag from the trolley and gestured, "This is the suite of Mr and Mrs van Diederijk. Your room, ladies, is across the hall."

"What brings you to Toronto?"

"Would you believe it if I said the University of Toronto orthopaedic surgery research hospitals?" he asked, standing only a breath away from her.

"Yes, I would."

"I would not," Sarre said, settling his arms around Alethea, "My darling wife draws me here; the university hospitals are an added bonus. Most importantly, I wanted to tie up loose ends, so to speak," his right hand hovering at the knot of his towel.

To the other people hovering, he announced without ceremony, "A change of plans if Alethea will consent. I visit orthopaedic surgery clinics and deliver a couple lectures at the university while you are at the convention. And after tomorrow, my dear wife and I will be staying in other accommodation."

"Which floor, darling Sarre?"

He looked like a little boy who was proud to do something very right, "On the Toronto islands, my love, an island cottage all to ourselves, we have an entire week." Sarre showed photos on his mobile.
Alethea nestled against him, "Toronto looks beautiful at night from the islands. And after our island honeymoon, my love, we visit Granny. And make our way home to Huis van Diederijk…"
"Is that what you want? Are you ready to take the plunge again?" he asked for verification as everyone looked on approvingly, happy things were turning around, in a big way.

"Only with you, by my side," she murmured against his chest, stars in her eyes.

He had his hands with clear intent on the clasp of her skirt – at that sign they were superfluous, Philly and Sue, and the bellman scrambled for the exit at – and Alethea said hurriedly, "Oh, darling Sarre, you can't, not here."

"Can't I?" he asked her… and they did.

AND THEY LIVED HAPPILY EVER AFTER

2. The Right Kind of Girl – She's a Lady

This is an update of The Right Kind of Girl by Betty Neels

The Right Kind of Girl: She's a Lady! Part 1

When Sir Paul Wyatt, prominent surgeon, 40, walked into his thatched cottage in Lustleigh in the Exeter countryside, his wife, 25 year old Emma, turned around, saw who it was, flew to her feet and ran across to him in a flurry of animals.

"Paul, you're back from Chicago!" Her voice was hoarse, and her nose pink from constant blowing, and it was a silly thing to say but she couldn't hide her delight that he made it in just before 8:30 in the evening.

He closed the door behind him and stood leaning against it, and it was only then that she realized he was in a rage. His mouth was a thin hard line and his eyes were cold.

"What possessed you to behave in such a foolish manner?" he wanted to know. "Why all the melodrama? What are the ambulances for? Or the police for that matter? What is the name of heaven possessed you, Emma? To go racing off across the moor in bad weather, sending dramatic messages, spending the night in a Godforsaken camp. Ignoring Diana's pleading to wait and give her time to phone for help. No, you must race away like a heroine in a novel, bent on self-glory."

Emma said in a shaky voice, "But Diana –"

"Diana is worth a dozen of you."

It was a remark which stopped her from uttering another word.

For three seconds.

With her calloused left hand, Emma thumped her beloved's solar plexus. Now most people pack a whallop with their dominant hand but Lady Wyatt proved emotions even things out.

"How dare you talk to me like that? Accuse me of grandstanding? You listened to her and you believed her without even asking me. Well, go on believing her, you've known her for years, haven't you? And you've only known me for months; you don't know much about me, do you? But I expect you know Diana very well indeed.'

Paul put his hands in his pockets. 'Yes. Go on, Emma.'

"All lies from that bloody Diana Pearson!" she added bitterly. "I was stuck on the moors with no mobile phone, nothing but prayer. I prayed and prayed that I would stay alive in that horrible weather so I could tell you how much I love you. I was so scared I would die frozen without telling you the truth. That bloody awful witch probably wanted me to die of exposure… and those babies too!"

Sobbing, Emma buried her face into her hands in despair…
Reaching for her, Sir Paul was taken aback all the same. Not by the
innocuous torso punch, but with joy at her words. She loved him!
He had been patient for weeks since their wedding…

"Oh, my darling Emma…" was cut off when she broke into the
most gut wrenching keening cries.

"You were the one who foisted me on that heartless woman…!
You are an absolutely beastly husband. I don't know why I love
you…! I should hate you!" she was in full roar.

"Emma," begged Paul, startled by her sudden loss of composure,
"I love you so much but you are making yourself sick…!" He
grabbed at her arms to stop her flailing.

She tore out of his grasp, "YOU are making me sick – Diana
throwing me onto the moors at night in the middle of winter is
making me sick. Your idea of 'love' makes me sick!" And headed
to the door, yanking it open, regardless of the cold weather,
heedless of the dark, and ran out like the Furies were chasing her.
Shod only in court shoes, no coat, tears running down her face,
sobbing, Emma only wanted to escape as quickly as possible
all her misery.

Paul chased after her in the night, finally catching her arm. She
whirled around, desperately trying to jerk free, "Let me go! I have
to go! I cannot stand this for another second!"

He implored his frantically struggling, distraught wife. "Emma, my
darling love, I do love you, please, I was so afraid to tell you
earlier…"

And she feverishly pushed against him, again and again in
response. He could not help but grunt and wrapped both arms

around Emma who was shouting, "That bloody woman has been trying to drive us apart… I can see it, why can't you? No, you believe every word from her!"

Paul felt gutted, he had behaved so badly towards Emma… "My darling, I am so sorry… I should not have listened to Diana, I was just so fearful of your safety. I trust you. Of course you wouldn't… I am so sorry, please forgive me."

This muffled against her hair as he held her quaking body, as she sobbed from the ordeal of the past 36 hours, forlorn, "Safe? I don't feel safe with you. Especially now. I hurt, Paul, you hurt me so bad. How could you say such cruel things to me?"

When he could feel the volcanic eruption of emotions die away like coal embers, within him travel worn by jet lag and her suffering from living under the roof of a distant and unfeeling new husband, each charge met with his soft-spoken apology and assurances to love openly and better, fifteen minutes of him holding her, keeping her warm, Paul gently carried his sniffling wife inside the cottage, Mrs Parfitt softly closing the front door behind him.

Muffled but audible, "You said that she is worth a dozen of me. You must secretly believe that, Paul, that I am not even a tenth of Diana…" He sank down with her in the large armchair by the fire, where the dogs bore silent witness to the pitiful sight of their mistress, weary emotionally and physically, limp and too past caring.

"Lady Wyatt has been fighting a cold and a sore throat since this morning when she rescued the babies, sir," intoned Mrs Parfitt. The reproach in Mrs Parfitt's voice was barely sheathed as she silently brought in a fresh pot of tea. If it had been iced lemon tea, he knew she would have tipped it over his head. Paul also felt the gaze of the Jack Russell and Labrador on him, censor in their eyes.

On the other hand, Queenie turned her back on him, disgust in her entire feline demeanour.

What kind of man would reduce the kind and gentle Emma to a dispirited puddle of tears? he cast his eyes down in shame…

Eventually Emma roused herself, clutching his handkerchief, looking calmly at him, "I lost control. I apologize…"

Then with resolve, Emma declared with resigned fortitude in her eyes, "Paul, it won't do for you to have a wife who is not good enough. This is good-bye – I should go pack now… The sale of Mother's house should be sufficient to keep me in kin and kith…"

Before Emma could extract herself from his lap, Paul came to a decision, "You are staying where you belong… I am an absolute rotter and I shall apologize for uttering this rubbish for the rest of my days… It is I who am not good enough a husband to you… "

He raised her hands to his lips and kissed the palms reverently. At that, she reacted tiredly but with surprise and a sense of contentment warmed her bones.

"Look at me, my love. I once said that anyone who insults my wife insults me. Anyone who harms my wife… I shall speak to Diana in the morning. And then neither of us will ever see her again." He idly stroked her hair, "You have my word on it."

"Words…" she sighed, a tear seeping from her eye, "Paul, you don't talk. And I have been ever so lonely…"

Paul closed his eyes against her obvious pain, "Never again, my love, will I make you feel that way. We start afresh." He gave her a gentle kiss, as their fierce storm passed as if it were shooed away by angels.

Later, after paperwork that needed his urgent attention and a shower, Sir Paul strolled silently along the passageway to check on his wife. Softly easing himself into her room, he gazed down on Emma slumbering in the shadows of the nightlight, an haunted expression on her sleeping face. As he drew closer, it clenched his heart to see tears stealing down her cheeks and silent sobs as she tossed and turned. Obviously a nightmare, he sat on the bed, and softly bent down, unable to resist his husbandly duty to offer her some comfort and perhaps a means to lead her away from her troubled dream.

Hearing her snuffles diminishing, after several indefinable minutes, Paul began extracting himself from her arms. Emma, however, would have none of that, instead snuggling closer, and gradually, she roused from her sleep. Her eyes shone sleepily, her lips trembled with remorse, "I feel so ghastly I tried to hurt you, Paul... I don't want you to go. Please stay..."

This he felt he had to obey, his virago, his Emma, to soothe her troubled heart, "My own love, I forgive you dearly. Please find it in your dear heart to forgive my putting you through so much misery... We start afresh, with love...".

She glowed and trustingly, sleepily, turned into his embrace. It seemed like mere seconds later, her eyelids and her breathing sank gradually into peaceful repose. With a quiet sigh to the Divine in gratitude on his face, Paul shifted more comfortably against the pillows, aware that they were taking steps towards a rapproachement.

Part 2: The Right Kind of Girl – She's a Lady

Along the hallways of the Wyatt cottage trod Mrs Parfitt. She cherished the stillness of early morning when light shyly beckoned the gleam of the Aga, the elderly panes of the glass, the reassuringly solid wood polish. Even the scent of the kitchen garden and greenhouse tomatoes were favorable in the tiny hours of the day.

The downstairs telephone sounded shrill, the unwanted intruder of the morning… a call for Lady Wyatt. Most urgent. Muttering, Mrs Parfitt paced herself up to the room of the lady of the house, casting her thoughts back to the past two days, "Poor little lamb… a gentle creature like her could only be crumbled under a harsh taskmaster… or a difficult husband." She frowned, what could have possessed Sir Paul?

Mrs Parfitt knocked gently on Emma's door. No answer. She thought about Lady Wyatt's ordeal on the forbidding moors and the housekeeper's motherly heart grew concerned. Sniffles, cough, cold… better to check.

Opening the door, the good Mrs Parfitt peered in. Emma was lying there, no longer pale and troubled, instead breathing peacefully. Her head pillowed on her husband's chest.

Sir Paul lifted his head, "Mrs Parfitt?" Cleanshaven, it was obvious he had elected to return to his wife's side after completing his morning ablution.
"A telephone call, sir, urgent for Lady Wyatt. It is Miss Pearson, she was most insistent."

Abruptly, Sir Paul sat up, throwing back the bed covers and reaching for his dressing gown. "An opportunity presents itself …" Movement which had the unfortunate effect of dislodging the slumber of Emma. Who was tumbling off the precipice of the other side of the bed.

Only swift action on Sir Paul's part, lunging to grab a hold of her waist, prevented a hard crash onto the floor.

Emma opened eyes, looking balefully at her husband, leaning down on her.

"A thousand apologies, my dove, I have to go take this phone call."

Satisfied with this explanation, Emma gave him a sweet smile that set his heart racing and drifted back to sleep.

She did not hear Sir Paul say clearly to Mrs Parfitt, "I will not have Miss Pearson calling Lady Wyatt or visiting this house…" as the door closed on the two of them heading back downstairs.

**

About an hour later, Sir Paul thought, how nice to have a tranquil breakfast, as he was finishing his coffee. It seems as if his entire household is giving him another chance, from the approving smiles of Mrs Parfitt to the wagging tails of Kate and Willy. He turned his attention to the day ahead… but first he had to make a proper leave-taking of Emma.

About to rise from his chair, he sat as Emma rushed into the breakfast room, clad in his dressing gown. "Oh, Paul, I am so glad you are still here…" looping her arms around his head and gave him a morning kiss.

It was a most welcome, if most unsettling, new experience for him to be the recipient of Emma's rather effusive affections. Paul refrained from saying anything about his qualms about public displays of affection – he was on tenterhooks enough with his wife. He felt grateful enough that Emma was willing to turn the page and start over.

He caught himself, pondering, "I was set in my ways, a crusty old bachelor expecting her to adapt to me. I now have to consider us as 'us'. Without adapting to her, the 'us' may quickly devolve into 'solo'." And recalling how quickly she had thrown him over barely 12 hours ago, Sir Paul knew he had created his own vulnerability.

Some of this may be due to the age difference… Emma at 25 was almost a generation younger than him. As Emma showed no sign of keeping her morning affections brief, Paul thought of the wisdom of the approach 'Vive la difference'… and enjoy the boldness of his virago…

**

Emma smiled from the front door, Paul had to muster every iota of strength to tear himself away from her. And the comforts of home.

Now that she had Paul on notice, Emma went about her day in an affable manner, thankful that out of something hurtful could come about a new footing.

As was her habit, Emma went to St John's church to sit and say a few prayers, feeling the sharp grief over her mother's sudden death slowly dulling into gentle mourning, day by day. She gave thanks for Paul's safe return from his two weeks lecturing in the United States, and asked for guidance as the two of them venture forth in their marriage, in love. And she prayed for strength to do something she had never dared before.

***

It was after a full morning at the hospital and consultations with his private patients and the truth from the grapevine as to Emma's true role on the moors that Sir Paul turned his attention to the future. He was on sabbatical, he was newly married to a gentle and lovely and – as he found out – lively Emma, and he had gone about his work as if nothing had changed. Working all hours suited him when home was a place to potter around the garden and read and refresh and then head back out again. Now home was Emma, and she was unabashedly showing him what he was missing under the roof of the thatched cottage. He intended to change that, in a drastic manner.

But first, take care of Diana Pearson. How dare she abandon Emma to the elements – that very morning, Paul had made speedy arrangements for him and Emma to have the latest mobile phone which were now in his medical case. He seethed with rage at her lies about Emma – and how gullible he was to take her at her word. But then, he had not taken proper care around Emma, so that she could reveal who she really was. "All my fault, how could she, when I did not reveal my own adoration for her. Nor unbend enough for her to get to know me."

Parking the Bentley, Paul opened the front door and headed to Diana's office. From now on, there would be no more contact between her and the Wyatt's. He rapped on her office door, "Diana? It is Paul Wyatt…"

"Ooo, Sir Paul, " the door was opened by Maisie, looking exactly as Emma had described her. A hardy young widow who worked at the children's home, "Just in time…"

Puzzled, Paul found the door opened wider by a middle-aged police officer, Sergeant Palmer, a colleague of a former patient of Sir Paul's. "Ahh, Sir Paul, how good of you. The travellers are in the debt of Lady Wyatt, they wanted her to know. But how distressing for everyone about Miss Pearson's actions. Now that Lady Wyatt has reported to us the full extent of Miss Pearson's dereliction of duty, we have Miss Pearson in now for questioning – we do not hold to wilful and reckless endangerment of life and charges are pending…"

Paul left shortly afterwards – with the board deciding by phone on a temporary manager while they sought a replacement for Diana Pearson. On the drive home, Sir Paul pondered that he was aware of hidden depths within everyone. His gentle virago is no longer asking his permission – she is going ahead to do what is right, not waiting for rescue.

When he had first met Miss Emma Trent, there was no inclination that how much she had kept under wraps. He was quite looking forward to what she was going to unveil to him next.

PART 4. THE RIGHT KIND OF GIRL – SHE'S A LADY

The next morning, Emma started breakfast with her customary short prayer, keeping an eye on the clock for their drive into Exeter.

"A most pleasant way to recover from jetlag, morning with my wife…" observed Sir Paul Wyatt to his wife, demurely pouring his cup of tea, "I shall have to bring you with me every time I cross time zones…"

"I put you to sleep, dear?" was Emma's nonchalant reply.

"You give me the most pleasant dreams… "

Animal inhabitants Queenie, Kate, and Willy followed the vainly-trying-to-keep-pokerfaced Mrs Parfitt bustling out of the breakfast room… three was definitely a crowd…

**

In the car, under crisp blue skies, neatly dressed in a printed, fitted jersey dress, a light Burberry coat, and a jaunty hat on her lap, Emma brought up the topic of jetlag, "I think you are trying to tell me something," averred Lady Wyatt.

"I have been offered two lecture tours to choose from – one of 2 months in west coast Canada and America, and one of three weeks in Italy... I would like to take you to the opera on either tour. " "Hmmm, i think Canada and America now. After all when the babies come, we cannot very well lark across the pond at the drop of a hat..."

His virago brought up something that had been on his mind, the idea of extending the family, "I would very much like to have children with you."

Mournfully, Emma sighed dramatically,"If only Elmer Fudd did not keep getting in the way... 'Kill the Wabbit' indeed... Kill the Mood, that's more like it..."

She continued, waving a buttery leather-gloved hand, only half in jest, "Since it does look like that will not change... Maybe we should just make a booking for IVF, and be done with it."

The Rolls pulled over suddenly over onto the verge, and halted safely out of the line of traffic. Paul unexpectedly reached over, unfastened her sealbelt, then his, and fastened his hands around her waist, and pulled her inexhorably close, hoarsely murmuring in her ear, "We do not need IVF..."

Countless moments of frantic embrace and murmurings and combs yanked from hair... Firecrackers, sirens, Knock, knock... "This is the police, do you need roadside assistance...?"

**

Emma looked with satisfaction at having her hair styled to just brushing her shoulders, enough length to pin up and enough to wear down and be neat. Her nails done at the salon, her normal shape-and-buff to a gloss, no polish… She was certain the salon staff privately thought Emma arrived 'doing the Walk of Shame', instead of a permitted marital embrace on the side of a British carriageway. One that was kept within the bounds of propriety through the intervention of the Exeter police. In any event, she did not require much time to be put together.

Then it was off to the shops in order to purchase a gift for her in-laws whom they were visiting tomorrow in the Cotswolds for the weekend. The box of Belgian chocolates found – then it was off to find something suitable tonight's dinner party just down the road from their home. Mission accomplished, sent Sir Paul a text, "Dearest, I finally got the opium I wanted."
He almost dropped his mobile phone, seated in the lecture theatre, Opium? Had he driven his wife to drink… Once the selfie of her holding the YSL perfume showed up, he relaxed slightly. It would have seemed unusual for an English rose like Emma to wear an oriental scent, though now he quite enjoyed that on the bedsheets.

It was trendy to show up at smart dinner parties sporting leggings – but Emma did not see the point of it and looked around for knee-length and longer dresses. At each of the various shops, Emma tried on several dresses in the dressing room and took selfie photos in the mirror and send to her husband.

"Dearest, I like this colour – what do you think?"

"This dress has long sleeves…"

'Pity the length of this one.'

'At last, something with a higher neckline!'

To which Sir Paul finally had to put up a white flag, 'Emma, for the love of God, I have to deliver a lecture in 7 minutes.'

Her reply, 'Oh, what MUST you think of me?'

His response was a succinct, 'Minx.'

**

"Bei den Waltzersee..." Paul checked the missed-call that Emma
was sending, it was thankfully image-free SMS, just to say she was
on the way to the lecture hall.
To the colleagues speaking with him after his lecture, Sir Paul
answered their inquiry, "My wife added this ringtone to my mobile
phone. Ahh, there she is…"

With several carrier bags bearing the names of shops in the
Cathedral Quarter, and fresh from the salon, Emma looked vibrant
and appealing, all the more so because she was unconscious of it.
All eyes on her, she had eyes only on her husband.

"Ahh, the charming Emilia," sighed a visiting Italian colleague,
kissing her hand, and not letting go, "But signora, I would say
something sweet from Verdi would be so suitable to you. You are
joining Paolo here on the lecture tour? Let me introduce you to the
magnificence of Italian opera at La Fenice, la Scala…"

"Let me take care of that, Giuseppe…" broke in Sir Paul, barely
civil.
"You are such a sweet man, Doctorre Giuseppe, when you are
being so Italian, I can only say in the words of Norma… *In mia
man alfin tu sei…*"
Silent spectator, Paul found the idea of a lecture tour of Canada in
the dead of winter more appealing over one in Italy.

***

After lunch in Exeter, an organic insalata mixta with light balsamic vinegar, a freshly prepared dover sole with new broiled potatoes, finished with an in-house vanilla ice cream with a ribbon of salted caramel and raspberries, Paul drove them home, "Nothing scheduled but look for a lie-in all weekend, we can leave the dinner party early tonight," he said meaningfully.

"Paul, dear, you arranged for us to visit your parents, remember you said we are leaving at 8 AM?"

She hid a smile, as Sir Paul Wyatt expressed his feelings most forcefully, "What do I have to do to get time alone with you?"

Helpfully, Emma offered, "Why, what you always do, dear, you set your priorities and then you schedule it… And you do it so awfully well. Take last night, the calls came in from the hospital and you took each of them. You have made it known from the beginning that your work is #1 with you. And that everyhing else fits around that. The fact that I am in your top five makes me feel privileged…"

She had him sitting in deep thought.

***

A splendid time was had at the dinner party in Lustleigh, everyone knowing each other and everyone knowing Paul very happy that pretty Emma was his wife. No one was surprised the Wyatts left as early as was decently possible. Indeed it was almost expected.

Entering the cottage, Emma yawned prettily, "What a lovely dinner party but we have to retire now with that long drive tomorrow morning to your mother and father.

She turned to look searchingly at her husband, "Umm, darling, don't come up to my room tonight…"

Paul's eyes narrowed, "Emma, I understand that my work interrupting us last night and today may have annoyed you but I was infinitely left more frustrated and remained so for a considerably longer period of time…"

Emma's eyes sparkled, "Paul, dear, just so that you do not misunderstand me, I was referring to the fact that tonight I shall test out the comfort of your bed. For sleeping purposes. I am old fashioned in thinking that a proper husband and wife share the same room. That way either I move to your room or you into mine, only one will be ours from now on.

"However, if you find that my presence would crowd you, please let me know now," she winked to diffuse the situation, "Will you be long?"

Paul, eager to get onto a better footing with Emma, replied, "As soon as I make several phone calls. I am without doubt that you will make my bedroom our bedroom. For sleeping purposes. You will bring the Opium…?"

Drifting off on a waft of scent, she assented, "I am beginning to see where we are on the same page."

Sir Paul made several phone calls and sent messages, shifting things around, often ruthlessly so. Then with a gleam in his eyes, he made for the stairs.

PART 5. (FINAL) THE RIGHT KIND OF GIRL – SHE'S A LADY

Fresh from her bath, swathed in her purchase from Chantelle, Emma was trying to get comfortable in the huge bed in the master suite. She had La Traviata playing softly in the background and experimented with the left side of the bed. The right side like Goldilocks. Finally she decided it did not matter and snuggled in the centre, closing her eyes, Queenie obligingly at her feet.

Paul came in quietly, turned off the music, currently not enamored with Italian tragedic operas, preferring a portent of a happy ending. He unhesitantly scooped up an affronted Queenie, and deposited her outside of his bedroom, swiftly closing the door. And took his evening shower.

Roused from her sleep by the sound of the shower, Emma sat up against the pillows. Sir Paul emerged clad in a towel and an untied dressing gown. He strolled purposely and came to sit on the side of the bed. The first thing came to her mind, Emma stammered, "I am going to insist on duvets. These sheets are slippery and cold."

Paul was quite pragmatic, "This thing you are wearing looks slippery and cold too. I do find it extremely fetching. though I don't know why you even bother…"

Emma leaned forward and gave him a good-night kiss, "We have an early start to the Cotswolds, pleasant dreams…"

Sir Paul wrapped his arms around her, to keep her from putting more distance between them, "As to that, I have rescheduled my parents til next week. And reassigned all my clinics and hospital work until the end of the sabbatical. We are going to have a proper lie in.. "

Emma glowed, "You have been able to reassign your responsibilities so quickly?"

Paul winced, "It is my set of priorities that I have belatedly reassigned. For that I apologize, my love. As a bachelor, I chose to come and go as I please. Now I have a beautiful wife and it pleases me more to make us my top priority. All else has to fit around that."

"My work has to fit around us. I have decided to shift some of my responsibilities to the rest of the team and bring on newer members. Lecturing and researching and consultation such that I can spend uninterrupted time with my wife. And share her life. In a fortnight, we fly to Toronto and then Vancouver for the lecture tour."

Sir Paul gestured to their bed, "I am not prepared to keep you on hold with regards to 'this kind of thing' as you term it. They can call someone else – I'll not have any opportunity to hear 'Kill the Wabbit' til we depart.

Starting tomorrow afternoon, Mrs Parfitt has the week off. She can stock the larder in the morning…"

Delighted by his plans, Emma teased him, "Paul, dear, are you prepared to make the bed for an entire week?"

"As to that, our house has at least 7 bedrooms so one could choose to feel extremely lazy…"

***

That nightgown next made its appearance in the Cotswolds. Leaving an enormous pile of laundered bed linens for Mrs Parfit to fold, the now truly married couple made good time on the road to his parents' home.

Sir Paul had fibbed, offering excuses that Emma's cold had lingered to postpone their visit to his parents by one entire week. Taking tea, Emma went pink when her mother-in-law said, "Well, cold or no cold, I must say that marriage suits you, my dear."

Emma put down her coffee-cup down with care and wished she didn't blush so easily. Blushing, she felt sure, had gone out with the coming of women's lib and feminism, what that was exactly, Mrs Wyatt, being of an older generation, wasn't concerned with either and found the blush entirely suitable.

Paul found it enchanting.

***

The morning of his 50th birthday, Paul still could not believe his good fortune to have been so blessed by the enchanting virago. Emma had been up to do the school run, insisting on an after-breakfast a lie in.

They were heading to the Cotswolds where the grandparents and cousins awaited. After school ended. Plenty of time between now and then for their lie in.

Paul and Emma counted themselves fortunate that first-class schools were within commuting distance from their home. There was no reason for them to board – Emma was adamant about not sending the children to a useless posh co-educational public school with hijinks. Already each child already was planning to follow in their father's footsteps or another professional field.

Mrs Trent's cottage in Buckfastleigh stayed in the family being let out as Paul and Emma wanted each child to have a place of their own for later in life. Lady Wyatt enjoyed making her contributions to town life via the church and to home through managing the household accounts and the family. The Honorable Michael is named after Emma's late father, the Honorable Andrew after

Paul's father. Having set that pattern in motion, it was appropriate that the Honorable John received the masculine version of the late Mrs Trent's name. The pretty little girl suited the name the Honorable Teresa Wyatt to a 'T'.

Of course it was only in recent days that their father's further contributions to the field of medicine were again recognised – which goes to show that one can prioritise love and family and still make a mark on the world of one's chosen profession – and the Wyatt offspring could add The Honorable in front of their names. But the children thought it sounded too much like "The Horrible", they told Maisie, their occasional babysitter.

And Emma was back, parking the car, and they made their way upstairs. Opening the bedroom door. Queenie the cat slid in, hopping right onto the bed. Paul unceremoniously scooped up the moody cat, and put her outside, "Go find Kate & Willy. Go to Mrs Parfitt. Go away."

An arm around Emma, Paul was climbing obligingly under the duvet while Emma switched off his mobile phone. Having thoroughly denuded the master suite of children and animals, Elmer Fudd was the final one to be exiled forthwith.

AND THEY LIVED HAPPILY EVER AFTER

3. A Star Looks Down... and shines on Elizabeth

Inspired by A Star Looks Down by Betty Neels ->

"Miss? We are in private. You can please tell the truth."

She sipped at the glass of water with an ice cube floating, and shivered at the past few hours tossed at sea... Elizabeth Partridge sat in a comfortable armchair in this warm room in the hospital, where she had been taken to tidy up in the adjoining bathroom, in a clean generic set of clothes as her own were being cleaned somewhere in the police station or hospital.

Sitting back, smiling kindly, the police officers, one in her thirties, the other a stout grandfatherly type looked perfectly at ease, enabling her to relax.

"But here we need exactly what happened. And you know as a nurse the value of the truth in civic society. Please, tell us from the beginning, the truth..."

Eluzabeth looked at the opposite wall, seeing again the rough intimidating North Sea, resolved to shield the ringleader of the four, ten year old Dirk Thorbecke from adult wrath without withholding the truth from the authorities, "Dirk did not mean it… I mean.. It was only a childish prank…" Elizabeth muddled, "Just like he did not foresee the consequences climbing the rock cliff last month either…"

"You seek to protect the child because he does not think like an adult perhaps? It is understandable – we in the Netherlands do that too. And you have a kind heart. And a clean record on Interpol." Spoke the older officer admiringly.

The female officer joined in, "Let us assure you that In Dutch law, the age of criminal responsibility is from the age of twelve onwards. So this young fellow would not bear an arrest nor a criminal record… Ahh, you relax, Miss, that is good, we are getting, as you say, the truth unfolding." Almost as an attempt to change the topic, the officer probed, "See, what was this rocks about…?"

Elizabeth rambled a bit on her time with four Thorbecke children, life in the hospital, which the officers took an avid interest in, her rescue of Dirk Thorbecke and the others outside of Castle Cary, her growing unease with him over the past few weeks. All while the police were discreetly taking notes.

"What if I told you what we know?" Inquired the lady police officer, "And not from you… A pattern of young Dirk. Of lying and defiance. From the youngest excitable children, Alberdina Thorbecke, we learnt that the eldest wanted to have some fun, watching you attempt to swim. He untied the boat, according to Hubert. The boeier that the family did not give permission to use. The boat he had no knowledge of steering. The boat that was carrying you out to sea and to your certain deaths – this from Dirk and Marineka. That is a crime against property known as theft."

Elizabeth nodded in agreement, "But Alexander thinks differently. You heard him shouting at me. He said it was all my fault… I did have responsibility to look after the children…"

The lady officer waved her hand, "You were tasked with activities, not a spoiled boy wanting to make trouble and rallying the others to give you the slip. And frankly, you are a trained nurse, not a trained teacher…"

"And Mijnheer Alexander van Zeust is not a trained police officer. Nor is he the parent of the children. As such he has no standing. We have told him to calm himself and to bring the mother to us at this station."

"Mijnheer? Is he not 'baron' here in the Netherlands?"

The older man shrugged, "My priority is peace and order in this country and this station… And I put him in his place – a supposedly brilliant man who listens to the fairy story of a child blatantly lying and blaming a nurse of character is not worth my time."

Bemused at this peppery police officer, Elizabeth obligingly replied to all their questions. It took only a few minutes, and then he courteously took his leave. The lady officer gave Elizabeth several blankets and the doctor urged her to take a nap while they finished up their paperwork. She was to stay three nights to be monitored. The British consul had decided to help repatriate her back to England.

While she was sleeping, a storm broke in the police station.

The youngest three were in the care of a social worker as the police officers awaited Alexander returning with his sister. Much delayed by Mevrouw Martina Thorbecke's hysterics.

Young Dirk Theobecke was being questioned by peppery police officer and his team – and they made it known that witnesses, not Elizabeth Partridge, pointed out it was Dirk at fault. Dirk's attitude had initially been defiance and contempt – he told the officers the impression that he is 'adel' and that nobility status gives him special status for his actions... The uniformed man tersely clarified to Dirk that his uncle may be adel and his mother may be adel but his father is not. And in this country, if he bothered to study history in school, he would realize that Dutch nobility is transmitted only through the father. And Dirk Theobecke was a commoner.

Even if Dirk were adel, that means nothing in criminal investigations. He is simply a spoiled boy who will be held accountable. He was caught stealing and liable for damages from when the stolen boat that sideswiped other yachts.

Drily, the officer added that ramming the yacht belonging to a former minister of state was hardly the best choice of target.

By then, his mother had arrived, shaken. Martina and Alexander sought to keep this matter out of the press. Appearing to compromise to the embarrassed family, the officer in charge responded that it was largely out of his hands what the media would say although he agreed to vouch for the reality it should be seen as a childhood prank gone wrong. He emphasized that Dutch law provides for preventive approaches to juvenile delinquency – a term that made Alexander and his sister, Martina, squirm – the first would be that Dirk was to report to the Youth Care Agency for counselling. And enrollment in the STOP program with its requirement for the youth offender to make formal apologies... Moreover, the police would be obtaining a court order to appoint a family supervisor to monitor Dirk.

"The law protects juveniles from being criminally responsible for their actions, that is what I said,"the officer ended blandly, "But the child and family will be liable for damages caused by his actions. It may be in your best interest to quietly compensate rather than be sued."

The officer personally put through a call to Dirk Theobecke senior, informing him of the outcome, "Welcome home to you," he muttered, hanging up.

The four children, very subdued, were reunited with their mother and uncle. Dirk was not going to get away with it this time. Youth officer. Counselling. Family supervisor. STOP program.

Martina asked, "Where is Beth? I need her to see to the children's supper and bed tonight, my nerves are shot…"

"As to that, Mevrouw," replied a stone-faced lady officer, "Miss Partridge will remain in hospital to recover and then return to the UK. Here is my card, please forward her pay and luggage to us along with her airfare and transportation back to London. And her bonus for saving the lives of your children."

4. A Suitable Match – And He knows it

It is not often that Sir Colin Crichton was in the operating theatre on a Saturday at St Biddolph's but this was a rare case and his Registrar and housemen could learn something. Everyone chez Crichton London had something to do – Nanny was supervising the maths homework of Teddy & Oliver, his boisterous nephews, not their favourite way to spend a Saturday morning. An incentive to master their respective maths topics was the imminent return of their parents for Christmas holidays.

Peter and Sadie called weekly from rural Brunei and on their last call on Sunday evening, plans were quite advanced to visit her parents at the Kennedy's home in Richmond and at Mrs Crichton's in Castle Cary over the Christmas holidays. Teddy innocently suggested to his mother that she gift a durian fruit to Grandmother Kennedy. An idea that was an insider's joke with his brother.

His home was meticulously run, to support his work in surgery, every facet of his life was arranged around his work and his patients. As he was about to start, there was something about this

Saturday patient that caught Sir Colin's attention, and he decided it needed to be checked out before proceeding further.

Sir Colin had to stop by his consultant office and decided to drop the covered kidney dish off at the path lab along the way. Everyone at St Biddolph's – from the cleaners to medical staff and nursing to members of the Board of Governors – thought highly of Sir Colin, he was considerate that way, knowing the hospital was operating with a skeleton staff on the weekends. Entering the path lab area, he was taken aback to see an unexpectedly pretty female member of staff in the St Biddolph's pinny.

This young woman was blessed with a beautiful face and an impressive bosom.

He stopped in front of her. "Ah, splendid, get this checked at once, will you, and let me have the results? I'll be in the main theatre. It's urgent." He handed her a covered kidney dish. "Do I know you?"

"No," replied the heavenly creature in a melodic, public-school voice.

Sir Colin, curiosity sparked by the incongruity of her accent and her employment situation, made a note to find out who she was. It was obvious that she had no clue who he was, which was in itself unusual to him.

Upstairs in the main operating theatre, he gowned himself for the intricate surgical procedure that was imminent, prepared his team and residents for the work ahead of them. The medical students were silently thanking God they would witness this esteemed consultant at work – and his patients should be thanking their lucky stars too. In hopes that the path lab would send the same staff up with the specimen, Sir Colin then set out.

Just in time, he took the kidney dish from her with a nice smile. "Good girl – new, aren't you?" He turned to go and then paused, having noted the absence of any rings on her left hand, inquired almost nonchalantly, "What is your name?"

"Eustacia Crump." She flew back through the swing doors, not wanting to hear him laugh, everyone laughed when she told them her name. 'Eustacia' and 'Crump' didn't go well together. He didn't laugh, only stood for a moment more watching her splendid person, swathed in its ill-fitting overall, nevertheless giving shape and definition to match the view from the front, disappear.

It was a tricky few hours for the first patient – and then a short break before the last surgery of the day. Sir Colin took in some fresh air to clear his mind and was heading back when Miss Eustacia Crump stood there waiting for something, obviously having delivered the much-needed vaocliter of blood.

"Brought the blood?" he asked pleasantly, and when she nodded, "Miss Crump, isn't it? We met recently." He stood in front of her, apparently in no haste.

"Tell me," he asked, "why are you not sitting on a bench doing blood counts and looking at cells instead of washing bottles?"

It was a serious question and it deserved a serious answer. "Well, that's what I am – a bottle washer, although it's called a path lab assistant, and I'm not sure that I should like to sit at a bench all day – some of the things that are examined are very nasty…"

Miss Eustacia Crump was a delight, forthright, well-brought up… a stunning woman, probably the first he has seen in a long time without makeup looking so appealing.

His eyes crinkled nicely at the corners when he smiled. "They are. You don't look like a bottle-washer…"

"Oh? Do they look different from anyone else?"

Sir Colin didn't answer that one but went on, "… you are far too beautiful," he told her, and watched her go a delicate pink.

A door opened, and the odious nurse came back with the path lab form in her hand. When she saw Sir Colin standing with Miss Crump, she smoothed the ill humour from her face and smiled.

"I've been looking everywhere for you, sir. If you would sign this form…" She cast Eustacia a look of great superiority as she spoke. "They're waiting in theatre for you, sir, " she added in what Sir Colin considered an oily voice.

Annoyed at the nurse for interrupting his conversation with Miss Crump, Sir Colin took the pen she offered and scrawled on the paper and handed it to Eustacia. "Many thanks, Miss Crump," he said with grave politeness. He didn't look at the nurse once but went back through the theatre door without a backward glance.

Before turning his full attention to his patient, Sir Colin reflected on his schedule, booked up solid with consulting, private patients, surgical works until mid-December, then Christmas holidays. He would have to follow up with Miss Crump in the new year.
***

Miss Grimstone, Sir Colin's housekeeper and cook, sat in the bright kitchen with a teacup in her hand the following Saturday, while lunch burbled on the Aga. Grimstone, her brother, had just left to meet Nanny at the train after her visit to her mother.

She was looking forward to a return to having in residence the only Crichton who did not hurl rugby footballs in the hallways when it rained. And left action figures in their rooms at tea time. Teddy and Oliver Crichton, the young nephews, were definitely the 'chip off the old block', pondered Rosie, as she remembered younger versions of Colin and Peter dodging around the Grimstones with similar antics. And soon, for the better period of a fortnight, the Crichton house would revert of his bachelor's quarters.

So Rosie was in this house, drinking in a few hours of tranquility.

Mindful of the mental health needs of his household staff, Sir Colin decided to give his house and its vulnerable table lamps a respite from the juvenile energies of his nephews. He decided Saturday morning was an ideal time to give them their head – take them to Kew Gardens like Peter and Sadie used to.

He thought about the previous Saturday meeting the path lab assistant and wondered how someone of her bearing, someone whose erect carriage pointed to debutante balls and waltz lessons for giggling 8 year old girls was washing bottles in the path lab.

In the crisp November sun, also walking near the Orangerie, the Crichtons spotted an elderly man dressed with attention to detail, a hat, leather gloves, accompanied by a young woman in her early 20s. There she was again, Miss Eustacia Crump.

Beautifully mannered, she introduced her grandfather, Mr Henry Crump, to them. The boisterous boys had someone else to speak with, Miss Crump, while Sir Colin could have adult conversation of a non-medical sort with the agreeable and well-informed Colonel Henry. They shared similar tastes in books and architecture – and he gathered that Eustacia did too.

The boys were enjoying her calm but vibrant personality. As Teddy & Oliver kept sharing about the horrible maths, their opinion of school, the latest amusements, Sir Colin suppressed a wish to be 21 years younger, and speak to her honestly and openly as his nephews, and look upon her with wide-eyed admiration. As it was, Colin had to remind himself sternly, he was a professional man, no longer a boy.

The Crump family lived in a ground-floor flat in Kennington, a rather salubrious part of London, and Sir Colin bundled everyone in to drive them back from Kew Gardens. "We have enjoyed your company, " he told Eustacia with a smiling gaze, "They like you."

He left out that he too liked Eustacia.

Then Sir Colin drove the Rolls smoothly home, handing over the nephews to their Nanny. Shrieking young boys disturbed Rosie's quiet, as Teddy & Oliver rushed into the kitchen, eager to share their adventures and meeting the agreeable grandfather Crump and his granddaughter. Rosie hoped this time it did not include any more spiders…

Pouring himself a sherry in the drawing room, Sir Colin said to Moses, the dog, "That is that. She is an old-fashioned girl. And at age 22, Miss Eustacia Crump is too young for me to date."

He resolved to forget her.
*****
"Mmmpf!" Colin was heading into St Biddolph's to check with his registrar when a feminine full head of hair, and its owner, collided into him. The scent of her, familiar, as he glanced down.
Eustacia…

What a pleasant way to end the first Saturday in December…

"Going home?" he wanted to know gently.

Eustacia nodded and then said, "Oh…" when he took her arm and turned her around.
 "So am I. I'll drop you off on my way."

Colin saw she was reluctant, "But I'm wet. I'll spoil your car."
"Don't be silly," he begged her nicely, "I'm wet too." He bustled her into the car and settled her into the front seat and got in beside her.
"It's out of the way," sighed Eustacia weakly.

"Not at all – what a girl you are for finding objections." They sat in comfortable silence as he turned the car in the direction of the river and Kennington.

That he had only just arrived at the hospital intent on having a few words with his registrar, when he saw her, was something he had no intention of revealing. He wasn't at all sure why he had offered to take her home; he hardly knew her and although he found her extremely pretty and, what was more, intelligent, he had made no conscious effort to seek her out.
It was a strange fact that two people could meet and feel instantly at ease with each other – more than that, feel as though they had known each other all their lives. Eustacia, sitting quietly beside him, was thinking exactly the same thing.

Sir Colin smiled nicely when she thanked him, got out of the car, opened the gate for her, and waited until she had unlocked the door and gone inside before driving himself back to the hospital, thinking about her. She was too good for the job she was doing, and like a beautiful fish out of water in that depressing little street.

He arrived back at St Biddolph's and became immersed in the care of his patients, shutting her delightful image away in the back of his mind and keeping it firmly there.

***

"Her name is OO-Stay-see-ah," said Teddy.

Oliver demurred, "Miss Crump is EU-Stay-see-ah."

Peter and Sadie were back for Christmas R&R in London and keeping busy as Nanny was taking more time off with her mother. While Sadie was getting the full story from the boys about their meeting a very nice young lady and her friendly grandpa, Peter absentmindedly looked at the collection of a Christmas cards on the mantle in the drawing room.

There was one from Fryslân in the Netherlands – a family of 6 with the lady of the house wearing a long pink organza gown, the eldest son holding a cat, obviously the feline was the deputy master of the house.

Sadie helped the boys with the Christmas tree ornaments, "Then we must send your new friends something for Christmas. Do you think a large box of chocolates, homemade, would be sufficiently festive for Mr Crump and his granddaughter?"

To their chorus of assent, Sadie added this to her list of shopping before they drove off to Richmond. She felt grateful that there was someone who took time to be kind to her sons in London.
The next day, Sadie found it surprisingly easy to arrange for this box of treats, covered with brocade and red ribbons, to be dropped off St Biddolph's hospital.

Colin said he would personally make sure it would be ready for Eustacia to bring home after her shift on Christmas Day.

Later, Christmas Eve in Richmond, as Sadie was tucking in her sons to bed at her parents' home, she asked the boys, "Oliver and Teddy, would you say Miss Crump is pretty?"

Teddy, who was learning synonyms in school, piped up, "Oh, Eustacia is pretty, lovely, beautiful, fetching, appealing, youthful, belle, eye-catching…"

"I think you have your answer, dear," murmured Peter.
***

Part 3: A Suitable Match – And He Knows It
"I wish Mommy were here…"

Sir Colin Crichton held his younger nephew, Teddy, as the 8 year old sniffled in between barking hacking coughs, and he silently agreed.

It has been quite a fraught beginning of the year. His sister-in-law, Sadie, and his brother, noted architect Peter Crichton, no sooner jetted back to his latest project in Brunei a day after Boxing Day than Nanny received word about her mother. Immediately, Nanny left the boys for good after years with them in order to provide care for her own ailing parent for an indefinite period of time. As the Christmas holiday season was quiet and school was imminent, Sir Colin, Rosie Grimstone, and her brother, Grimstone, together kept up the boys' routine just fine.

This plan, as the Americans would say, got 'shot to hell' when Oliver first, then Teddy came down with the tonsillitis and flu, which developed into chest infections, specifically, the bronchial type. The hacking cough that keeps the patient up at night. And consequently, kept up Sir Colin and the Grimstone siblings awake what with ferrying soothing cool drinks, restocking boxes of tissues, administering pain relief medication, and holding onto little boys sitting pitifully in large beds. The next four days saw Miss Grimstone's meals devolving from par excellence to par-for-the-course and Grimstone appearing looking like he was in his 80s rather than his late 60s, and Sir Colin returning home from a day of consultations, operating theatre, private patients, to hours by the bedside of his nephews, before catching a few hours of sleep. His dates were not always understanding.

When it became obvious that this could not go on, Sir Colin engaged a private nursing agency to work in shifts in caring for the boys. Two times a day for three weeks, a revolving door of competent nurses rang the doorbell of Sir Colin's home to look after the medical needs of the two young patients. Bewildered by the parade of new faces, the lack of constancy impeded the boys's recovery and return to school.

Now Sir Colin had a situation in which the boys were not well enough to go back to classes but fit enough to be out of their beds. In a wintry windy London, the boys could not be outside so their venue for horseplay often had vases, scones, family photo frames bearing silent witness to their antics. The decorative arts 'road kill count' was increasing, as a result.

There had to be a solution, Sir Colin thought, as he roamed through the corridors of St Biddolph's… A staff wearing the pinny of the path lab passed him – Sir Colin turned to see it was not the delightful Miss Eustacia Crump. Whom he had been assiduously avoiding. And then an idea came to him.

The boys needed to be away from London, and they always loved the family home in Turville. It would be an ideal village setting for their recuperation. The Samways were always there.
Unfortunately, it was a wee bit too far for him to commute daily from London. The boys needed a father figure at home, not alone with household staff – and Sir Colin was too preoccupied with his work to offer his nephews much in the way of that.

When he and Peter were growing up, they thrived under the watch of their Grandfather Crichton – and Sir Colin thought Colonel Henry Crump would be of service. Mr Crump was living on his military pension, in reduced circumstances in Kennington, and Colin knew the elderly gentleman still had masses of wisdom to share. The Crump family came from rural stock, as such, it would be welcome return to their roots.
The retired colonel could be persuaded to go to Turville, although chances are Mr Crump would refuse to leave his granddaughter to live in a questionable part of London by herself. Colin could be quite ruthless when stakes were high, and in this case, the wellbeing of his nephews and the imminent jeopardy to his own work. He needed Mr Crump, and if that meant Eustacia had to be persuaded, so be it. With Peter confiding that agreement for a

74

multi-year extension to the Brunei project needed only a couple more signatures, the boys required the ongoing guidance of a father figure. They would also get the bonus of an honorary aunt in the form of Miss Eustacia Crump.

Sir Colin decided to frame it as the boys needing a governess and that meant Miss Crump. Mr Henry Crump would naturally be part of the package deal. Peter and Sadie decided to more than treble Eustacia's current salary as path lab assistant. With room and board on top of Eustacia's wage, the total compensation package for the balance of year 1 could hardly be refused by someone with good sense.

By the time Peter & Sadie returned for good in five years' time, the Crumps would have accumulated a sizeable nest egg and very good references. Eustacia Crump would be much further ahead than if she had stayed in the path lab. Now it was up to Sir Colin to put his plan into place.

First, he had to make sure Eustacia was at St Biddolph's on the afternoon he would visit Mr Crump. Once Colonel Henry Crump was on board, it would be a fait-accompli for Eustacia to agree to.

It was past the middle of January when Colin drove in from Turville, parked the car in front of the Crump flat in Kennington, bearing a hamper of sandwiches, jam, fruit, and a carton of coffee. The door opened, "Sir Colin! Do come in," beckoned Mr Crump.

***

That Sunday, a self-satisfied Sir Colin closed the boot of his Roll, helped Mr Crump into the front, tucked away Eustacia into the back seat, and contently headed to Turville. He had pulled every string he had at St Biddolph's, with the personnel department agreeing to take Eustacia back whenever she finished up with the Crichtons.

Although her beauty trespassed onto his thoughts all too often, Sir Colin put her deep into the background – in the end, Eustacia Crump was an old-fashioned girl of 22 and that was that.

One week later, Samways answered the phone. "Sir Colin Crichton's residence," and then, "Good evening, sir. Yes, Miss Crump is here."Samways smiled again as he handed the phone to Eustacia.

Sir Colin's voice came very clearly over the line. "Eustacia? You don't mind if I call you that? The day has gone well?"

"Yes, thank you, sir. They have been very good and they went to bed and to sleep at once." She gave him a brief, businesslike resume of their day. "I told Mrs Crichton when she phoned not to worry – the line from the Far East was frightful but she understood clearly. But Sir Colin, they both cough a great deal…"

"Don't worry about that, that should clear up now they're away from London. I'll look them over when I come down. You and your grandfather have settled in?"

"Yes, thank you. Grandfather has just gone to his room. I think he is a very happy man, sir…"

"And you, Eustacia?"

"I'm happy too, thank you, sir."

"Good, and be kind enough to stop calling me sir with every breath."

"Oh, very well, Sir Colin. I'll try and remember."

He sounded as though he was laughing as he wished her good night and rang off.

Things were going according to plan, the boys were happy with the Crumps in residence in Turville, and he could turn his full attention back to his research, consultation, patients, and upcoming lecture tours that year. And his own private life…

Sir Colin had phoned on Saturday morning to say that since he had an evening engagement, he wouldn't be down until Sunday morning after they returned from church.

"I expect he's going to take Gloria out to dinner," said Oliver.

The young nephew was half right. At this very moment, Grimstone was bringing to the guest room the overnight bag of Miss Gloria Devlin.

Part 4: A Suitable Match – And He Knows It
Updating TGB's A Suitable Match

Gloria Devlin knew they made a striking pair – heads turned to admire her arm in Sir Colin Crichton's as they made their way from the gala performance. Minor royalty were introduced to the prominent surgeon. In the Court Circular, it is, by quirk and tradition, listed the other way around, but in reality, it is the decorous royal wife who is honoured to be presented to such a dedicated and renown medical professional, knighted so young for his work in surgery.

The talent and experience in those hands and fingers of Sir Colin, Gloria could only let her eyes graze, her companion having masterly control of the powerful Rolls. Quietly and with purpose, the iconic British car was making its way back to his house in that part of London where the arts and Michelin restaurants and shop windows had little contact with graffiti and state comprehensives. As January was coming to a close, the air was refreshingly nippy, beckoning Gloria's fur stoll to serve a useful purpose on top of backdrop to her image as a carefree woman about town.

"A light supper is served for you, Sir Colin," sedately intoned Grimstone as he took their outer coats and her evening bag. "And the fire nicely keeping tonight's chill at bay…"

Sir Colin saw Gloria to her seat, and they savoured Rosie's fresh melon with prosciutto, smoked Canadian salmon on a bed of organic lettuce, and delicate strawberries and raspberries accompanied by an AOC white Cabernet Sauvignon from the Val de Loire region.

In the drawing room, Gloria was recounting an improv by the lead soprano, needing the programme from the evening's performance, which was in her evening bag. Colin asked Grimstone, who had been serving and was about to retire for the night, to fetch the bag.

The house telephone rang – Gloria was of the opinion that telephones should be barred from weekend dates, coaxing Colin, "Do be a dear and do not pick up, let your manservant take it and leave a message you are not available…"

Laughing, Sir Colin had already picked up the phone, "In your world, my pet, that is utterly expected, let me chase whoever it is away to call the next person on the list. I intend to be very occupied tonight…"

The receiver halfway to his ear, Gloria pressed herself against Colin, "I think highly of that…"

Tantalizingly distracted, Colin informed the caller, "Crichton…"

The line was muffled, "Mr. Colin Crichton? I am calling you from Bandar…"

Being called "Mister" brought Sir Colin back three years, it had been that long since. Bandar something or another? He did have a recent patient from the Gulf called Prince Badir…

"Badir, His Highness Prince Badir…?" Colin recalled that the operation was a success and now the prince's care was in the hands of his cardiologist.

"Uhh, sorry, no, not a person 'Badir'… The city…"

The speaker had a distinctly un-British accent. Probably a call from America, a suburb of Milwaukee or Baltimore or some place like that. Impatient, Colin wanted to get back to matters at hand with Gloria, "I am afraid I do not follow, perhaps if you could…?" Get to the point, Colin wanted to say but he had been brought up properly.

Gloria could act like quite a slapper and entwined herself around Colin, all enticing.

"This line is unfortunately not clear, Mr Crichton, I am calling you from Bandar Seri Begawan, the capital of Brunei. Your brother, Peter Crichton, held the architectural project…"

His hand over the receiver, Colin admonished Gloria, "Moss Devlin, you are killing me with that, do be a good girl and let me finish getting this person off the phone and on his way…"

"…instantly in their vehicle. We are so sorry to inform you," the speaker continued.

Colin put the receiver up to his ear again, "Sorry, what was that again? You are calling from Brunei, yes, please put my brother through to me."

"Mr Crichton, this line has gotten fuzzy again and you did not hear me just now. This is regarding your brother, we cannot put him on the phone. Just an hour ago, there was a tragic accident on the road and there were some injuries and casualties. We are sorry to inform you that your brother, Peter Crichton and his wife, Sadie Crichton were among the casualties."

Sir Colin shook his mind clear, "What? Can you repeat that? Are you saying my brother and sister-in-law…"

"They would not have suffered. Instant. They would have not felt a thing…" and the functionary continued on, moving to issues of making arrangements.

Pale, Colin put his hand over the receiver, half listening to the speaker at the other end, "Gloria, this is a call from Southeast Asia, Peter and Sadie are dead in a road accident…"

Gloria rolled her eyes, "Let this not spoil our evening. We can just go upstairs and it will be still there in the morning to deal with. Foreigners, why can't they have the decency to wait until Monday?"

***

"Grimstone, can you bring Miss Devlin's overnight bag down from the guest room?" Keeping his face as bland as possible, and tampering down his bubbling outrage, Colin turned to his evening companion, "My dear, as you so accurately guessed, this… news had altered things inexorably for me. I have now become the de facto father of my two nephews. My time and my life are no longer

80

my own. Grimstone, can you please bring around the car? I will take about five minutes to inform my mother in Castle Cary."

Colin closed the door, sat down in the huge wing backed chair, and closed his eyes. He needed a minute to rest, to give a brief minute for the work ahead – to speak to his mother, to break the news to the boys, to bring back Peter and Sadie. An Americanism came to mind, he had to put his Big Boy pants on… For the first time in his life, a family tragedy to deal with. He had to be the head of the family. And he felt alone.

After breaking the sad news to his mother by phone, leaving behind a haggard Grimstone, Colin immediately drove Gloria home – disgruntled, she saw no reason for the interruption of their evening plans. After seeing her safely to her flat, very cordially making apologies for the change of plans, Colin concluded that that was that for Gloria. Being fey was charming for a happy-go-lucky person but Colin was disappointed that there was no other side to her.

He was about to head back to his London house – his carefree bachelor days were over – in reality, long over as his interludes and lady friends had already been hardly worth the bother – Peter and Sadie had discussed with him his guardianship of his two young nephews in the unlikely event anything were to happen… when Sir Colin paused with key in the ignition.

Only a half hour drive at this time at night, it occurred to him. In thirty minutes, he could be with the gentle beauty who cared for young boys and old grandfathers and cats and dogs and the country life… He picked up his mobile phone and dialled Turville, he wanted to hear Eustacia's voice.

It was midnight but she picked up. "Is there something the matter? Is something wrong?"

"Very wrong. I'll tell you when I get home." Sir Colin asked her to wait up. She unhesitantly agreed.

He put his head into his hands – Peter. His partner in crime forever. His only sibling…

After a quarter of an hour, Colin got his composure back and started the car. Heading home.

***

Eustacia shuffled around the kitchen, peering in cupboards looking for biscuits – he would probably be hungry. She had just found them when she heard the car, and a moment later, his quiet footfall coming along the passage towards the kitchen.

He was wearing a dinner-jacket and he threw the coat he was carrying on to a chair as he came in. He nodded to her without speaking and went to warm his hands at the Aga, and when she asked, "Coffee, Sir Colin?" he answered harshly, "Later," and turned to face her.

It was something terrible, she guessed, looking at his face, calm and rigid with held-back feelings. She said quietly, "Will you sit down and tell me? you'll feel better if you can talk about it.

He smiled a little although he didn't sit down. "I had a telephone call just as I was about to leave my London house this evening. My brother and his wife have been killed in a car accident."

****

Eustacia look at Sir Colin in horror. "Oh, how awful – I am sorry!" Her gentle mouth shook and she bit her lip. "The boys… they're so small." She went up to him and put a hand on his arm. "Is there anything I can do to help?"

She looked quite beautiful with her hair loose around her shoulders, bundled into her dressing gown – an unglamorous garment bought for its long-lasting capacity – her face pale with shock and distress, longing to comfort him.

He looked down at her and at her hand on his arm. His eyes were cold and hard... with the superhuman force against enticing her into his arms and carrying her upstairs. This was why he drove her home from Kew, went out of his way to give her a lift on that rainy dark December Saturday, made time during a busy Christmas eve to have ready that enormous box of chocolates, why he moved heaven and earth to bring the Crumps to Turville. Eustacia with her vibrance, her kind nature, her ability to listen and to talk with a maturity beyond her years, her pleasing shape and eyes and beauty...

To find bliss in her arms in that huge bed in that large room upstairs, yes, how wonderful that would feel – that was not what the unworldly Eustacia intended... although he knew she would give him comfort of any sort if he was sufficiently persuasive... And he proved he could be, time and again.

Colin held himself back – he wanted Eustacia for the rest of his days. And for her to also feel the same. There were ways to bring about this delightful outcome, but to behave impetuously in 'life affirming' activities for the rest of the night with her, this was not the best way...

Eustacia – unaware of the pitched battle between responsibility and man-of-the-world primal urges coursing through every cell in his body – seeing only his eyes cold and hard, snatched her hand away as though she had burnt it.

PART 5: A SUITABLE MATCH – AND HE KNOWS IT

Updating TGB's A Suitable Match

Eustacia snatched her hand away as though she had burnt it and went to the Aga and poured the coffee into a cup. She should have known better, of course; she was someone filling a gap until circumstances suited him to make other arrangements. He wouldn't want her sympathy, a stranger in his home; he wasn't a man to show his feelings, especially to someone he hardly knew. She felt the hot blood wash over her face and felt thankful that he wouldn't notice it.

She asked him in her quiet voice, "Would you like your coffee here or in your study, Sir Colin?"

"Oh, here, thank you. Go to bed, it's late."

She gave a quick look at his stony face and went without a word. In her room she sat on the bed, still in her dressing-gown, going over the past half-hour in her mind. She wondered why she had been telephoned by him; there had been no need, it wasn't as if he had wanted to talk to her-quite the reverse. And to talk helped, she knew that from her own grief and shock when her parents had died. It was a pity that he had no wife in whom he could confide. There was that girl the boys had talked about, but perhaps he had been on his own when he'd had the news.

She sighed and shivered a little, cold and unhappy, and then jumped with fright when there was a tap on the door and, before she could answer it, Sir Colin opened it and came in.

It has taken the better part of half an hour for Colin to make amends to Eustacia. He had to first get a grip on himself and that took a combination of prayer and a shot of whisky from the drawing room. By then, she had gone to her room… so he poured himself some more whisky…

To her, Colin looked rigidly controlled, but the iciness had gone from his voice. "You must forgive me, Eustacia – I behaved badly.

I am most grateful for your sympathy, and I hope you will overlook my rudeness – it was unintentional."

She gave him a shy smile, "Well of course it was, and there's nothing to forgive. Would you like to sit down and talk about it?" Her voice was warm and friendly, but carefully unemotional. "It's the suddenness, isn't it?"

She was surprised when he did sit down. He was too, he had intended to apologize and make a quick retreat though speaking to her suddenly felt right. To think of his loss, rather than on her tucked inside her nightie, leaning against his pillows.

"I was just leaving the house – I had a dinner date – we were standing in the hall while Grimstone, my butler, fetched my – my companion's handbag. When the phone rang I answered it but I wasn't really listening; we had been laughing about something or other. It was a long-distance call from Brunei. Whoever it was at the other end told me twice before I realised…" He paused, and when he went on she guessed that he was leaving something out.

"I had to get away, but I wanted to talk about it too. I got into the car and drove here and I'm not sure why I phoned you on the way." He now knew why and the newness of it all still flummoxed him.

"Tell me about it," said Eustacia quietly, "and then you can decide what has to be done. Once that's settled you can sleep for a little while."

"I shall have to fly there and arrange matters." He glanced at his watch. "It is too late now…"

"First thing in the morning."

His smile shook her. "What a sensible girl you are. I have to tell the boys before I go." He looked at her. "You'll stay?"

"As long as I'm needed. Tell me about your brother and his wife."

"He was younger than I, but he married when he was twenty-three. He was an architect, a good one, with an international reputation. He and Sadie, his wife, travelled a good deal. The boys usually went with them, but this time they weren't too happy about taking them to the Far East. They were to go initially for three months and I had the boys – their nanny came with them but her mother was taken ill and she had to leave. Mrs. Samways has done her best and so has my cook, Miss Grimstone. It was most fortunate that we made your acquaintance and that the boys took to you at once."

"Yes. It helps, I hope. Let us say a prayer…" She beckoned Colin to kneel with her and led him with a few simple words.

"Now, we are going to the kitchen again and I'm going to make a pot of tea and a plate of toast and you will have those and then go to bed. When you've slept for a few hours you will be able to talk to the boys and arrange whatever has to be arranged."

"You are not only sensible but practical too."

It was after two o'clock by the time she got to bed, having made sure that Sir Colin had gone to his room. She didn't sleep for some time, and when she got up just after six o'clock she looked a wreck.

The boys were still sleeping and the house was quiet. She padded down to the kitchen and put the kettle on. A cup of tea would help her to start what was going to be a difficult day. She was warming the teapot when Sir Colin joined her. He was dressed and shaved and immaculately turned out, and he looked to be in complete control of his feelings.

"Did you sleep?" asked Eustacia, forgetting to add the "Sir Colin' bit. And when he nodded, "Good-will you have a cup of tea? The boys aren't awake yet. When do you plan to tell them?"

He stood there, drinking his tea, studying her; she was one of the few girls who could look beautiful in an old dressing-gown and with no makeup first thing in the morning, and somehow the sight of her comforted him. "Could we manage to get through breakfast? If I tell them before that they won't want to eat-we must try and keep to the usual day's routine."

"Yes, of course. May I tell Grandfather before breakfast? He is a light sleeper and there's just the chance he heard the car last night and he might mention it and wonder why you came."

"A good point; tell him by all means. Samways will be down in a few minutes, and I'll tell him. He was fond of my brother…" He put down his cup. "I shall be in the study if I'm wanted."

She did the best she could to erase the almost sleepless night from her face, thankful that her grandfather had taken her news quietly and with little comment save the one that he had heard the car during the night and had known that someone was up and talking softly.

Satisfied that she couldn't improve her appearance further, she went to wake the boys.

Meanwhile, Mr Henry Crump knocked on the door of the study. At Sir Colin's "Come in", the elderly gentleman went through to see Colin had made entries into his schedule.

"Son, Eustacia just informed me of the unfortunate news of your brother and his wife…"

Sir Colin looked up, the last time he had been called him 'son' by an older male in the family was his father before passing 2 years ago. From anyone else, it would have been received as an over familiarity.

"My granddaughter and I offer you our deepest sympathies, Sir Colin. While you are off to Brunei, know we will take good care of the boys," reassured the Colonel.

"Thank you, sir, may I hope to have that for even longer, an indefinite period of time after my return? I now have guardianship of the boys. If you have a few minutes before breakfast while I elaborate…?"

Briefly, the two men discussed how to go about telling the boys the sad news, settling them permanently in Turville, their schooling and continued daily lessons with the Colonel, the role of Eustacia, and the Crumps' place in his household. Sir Colin found it amusing that he found for Teddy & Oliver an honorary grandfather – and he himself acquired a respected and respectable father figure. From whose wisdom he would draw on in the years to come…

Mr Crump patted the younger man's shoulder as they went to breakfast, "My dear Colin, I think you are off to a good start."

***

Colin drove off after lunch to Heathrow. It would take him almost 20 hours after departing from Eustacia, arms around the shoulders of his tearful nephews, to checking into first class and connecting in Singapore to arrive in Brunei. He thought it wise to not rush Eustacia as it would be awkward if his strong primal feelings leaked out and she did not reciprocate, the cost to the boys' peace of mind was too great. Instead he would let her get used to life in Turville, of weekends getting to know him better, of taking her out, of coaxing her into seeing a future with him as appealing. After all he had time to do so and intended to make short work of it…

***

Almost a week later, he was back on the plane. The days in Brunei were full and exhausting with paperwork – this last morning was the most draining and paradoxically the most helpful. His final item on the packed agenda was a church service.

The Rector at St Andrew's had met his flight upon arrival and notified Colin of his congregation's insistence on the upcoming service. Colin did not feel the need for this ; still it was a mild concession to soothe local sensibilities.

"Ladies and gentlemen, this is Peter's brother, Sir Colin Crichton. He has a title like a Datuk because he is a very prominent surgeon in the UK."
Somberly, the ladies in colourful local attire explained what they had planned, "We will get you to your plane, Datuk Colin, first we shall have this service to say our farewell and thank you to Mrs Sadie and Mr Peter. Even though they were here just for a few months, their faith was strong. They spoke so well of you and their children and family. In our service we will have two hymns, one for them and one for you."

Sir Colin decided to bear with it, some would say it was a bit of an affront to have a hymn for him when no one here knew him aside from being the brother of Peter Crichton.

It was a familiar and reassuring service in the style of Church of England, as this Protestant church was part of the Anglican Communion. At the same time, it was up-to-date without being jarring.

He was moved by the prayers, the mourners speaking and indicating photos of Sadie and Peter participating in different events in the church calendar such as All Saints and Advent. They presented to Colin the different colour painted artwork that Teddy

& Oliver had sent to them in Brunei, and that were posted in the church school Sadie occasionally lent a hand to.

Each were added to a large envelope addressed to Colin's mother.

Colin glanced at several sheets of watercolours, one of which was in Teddy's distinct juvenile hand, "Oliver and I and Uncle Colin in Kew Gardens. We met a friendly grandfather called Mr Crump. He was walking his granddaughter, Miss Eustacia. We like her, she is like an Aunt."

At last, the Rector led the procession down the aisle, following the coffins of Sadie and Peter. The ladies right after held a photo of the couple smiling at a church function. The youngest choir member picked up a harmonica, and a boy of not more than 16 stepped up from the youth began to sing…

"The road is long
With many a winding turn
That leads us to who knows where
Who knows where
But I'm strong
Strong enough to carry him
He ain't heavy, he's my brother

So on we go
His welfare is of my concern
No burden is he to bear
We'll get there

For I know
He would not encumber me
He ain't heavy, he's my brother

If I'm laden at all
THEN I'm laden with sadness

That everyone's heart
Isn't filled with the gladness
Of love for one another

It's a long, long road
From which there is no return
While we're on the way to there
Why not share

And the load
Doesn't weigh me down at all
He ain't heavy, he's my brother

He's my brother
He ain't heavy, he's my brother…"

***

As the aeroplane lifted off, Sir Colin looked back on Bandar and
then thought of what fulfilling family life was ahead in Turville…
he hummed himself to sleep…

PART 6 FINALE **A Suitable Match – And He Knows It**

Realizing the name on the sheet of paper where Colin had written
the Groningen hospital where they were to meet for lunch did not
match that of the signage, Eustacia made her way rapidly towards
the correct location, knowing she was late meeting Colin for lunch.
Despite slingback pumps, Lady Crichton decided to pick up the
pace, now running, dodging university students without a care in
the world, shoppers with their bulky purchases, matrons buying

May flowers, cyclists paying no attention to pedestrians – she started running, while clutching her handbag.

Eustacia was beginning to panic, seeing she was 15 minutes late. Sniffing, she thought how could she be such a fool? Her first chance to be alone with her husband in over a week here in the Netherlands, the first chance since they were married 4 months ago, the answer to her prayers, and she could not get it right… Wiping a tear, she wanted to slap herself for getting lost in her daydreams…

Bam! She collided into a man, and apologized in Dutch, "He spijt me…"

"Where the hell have you been?" asked Sir Colin, and when she looked into his face, she saw he was angry – more than angry, in a rage.

She burst into tears.

"I am such a silly goose…I got lost – I don't know how that happened," she wailed, as he stepped forward and proffered a snowy handkerchief, and steered them into a quiet corner, "and I so wanted to be alone with you at last and now I have spoiled everything, Darling…"

"Did you say 'darling'?" Colin found it hard to believe his ears.

Eustacia was so distressed that she lost all restraint, "Since the night before our wedding, you have been my darling…"

Then she caught herself, "Oh, Colin, you weren't supposed to find out, I am sorry I know you want to keep this a 'mariage blanc' – oh, please forget I said anything…!"

Sir Colin responded by kissing her in a slow and most satisfying manner, and then quite roughly so that she found it impossible to speak, and when she would have done, "No, be quiet, dear heart, while I tell you how much I love you."

Just a stone's throw away from the crowds in Groningen historic square.

He smiled slowly and the smile soothed away the tired lines on his face. He said very clearly, "I have been in love with you ever since that first time – you wore a most unbecoming overall and I gave you a kidney dish. I didn't know it at the time, of course, I only knew that I loved you, that you were part of me, my heartbeat, my very breath. It seemed fate was to be kind to me when circumstances made it possible for us to marry but then I began to doubt... You are so much younger than I, my darling, and somewhere in this world, there must be a young man only waiting to meet you..."

Quite unexpectedly, two more large tears rolled down her cheeks. "Oh, pool, I don't much care for young men," she sniffed. "I thought you didn't care tuppence for me, so I tried to be what I thought you wanted me to be. And you never wanted to be alone with me all these weeks..."

"I didn't dare to be. But we are now. My dearest darling, we are now..."

"Oh, how very nice," said Eustacia, managing to say it before he kissed her again, "I'm so glad we're married."

She looked up into his face. His heavy lids had lifted and his blue eyes blazed down into hers. "And so am I..." he told her softly.

***

"I take it that staying at Haso and Prudence's place was one of my poorer choices in life?" Colin asked, his arm around Eustacia, murmuring into her hair.

"For lectures, how convenient. For a very newly-married couple, how very inconvenient..." affirmed a sleepy Eustacia, catching sight of the Martini Tower outside the window.

The Prinsenhof Hotel in downtown Groningen is listed in many guidebooks as the best hotel in the city. It certainly is convenient to the Market Square and most convenient for the only impetuous action by Sir Colin in recent memory. Without any prior reservation, walkin hotel guests usually pay the rack rate and find only the best rooms of the hotel available... Sir Colin merely handed over his credit card, Eustacia made a hurried grab for the room key, and they proceeded on their way.

Prinsenhof Groningen... A polite knock announced room service with lunch from the Restaurant Alacarte. Reluctantly, Colin reached for the hotel robe and padded over to the outer room of their suite to answer the main door. Covering her bosom with the duvet, Eustacia reached for the phone, and made a call to Prudence.

Their hostess was so delighted with how things have turned around that without hesitation, Pru noted to cancel tonight's drinks party for the Crichtons and also arranged for their luggage to be delivered forthwith to the hotel...

After Colin had taken care of room service, they called Turville, where Mrs Crichton was prevailed upon to stay a further two weeks. She was delighted at the joy and happiness in the voice of her son – very soon, Colin's workload will reflect his newly-married status and he would be living more or less full time in Turville. They would return home to find Teddy & Oliver showing off making their own beds and tidying up more after themselves. "Aunt Eustacia, we have even prepared the vegetable garden with Granny and Grandfather Crump," announced Teddy. Mr Crump showed them how to be self-sufficient men, trained as he was in army, and they were busy emulating him.

"And that is that," voiced Colin, hanging up, "Where do you think you're taking me?" as Eustacia emerged from under the bed covers and slipped on a robe and led him by the elbow.

Demeurely, she replied, "The shower, of course. I was trained at the path lab to go to lunch break with clean hands. I hope you get accustomed to it. That's what happens when one decides to marry a bottle washer…"

****

EPILOGUE

'This summer, Grandmother Crichton stayed with us for 3 weeks while Aunt Eustacia accompanied Uncle Colin on a lecture tour in Canada. We had been there two years before with Mummy and Daddy and we showed our family photos of the Rocky Mountains and western Canada.'

This was in the dutiful Christmas letter that Oliver and Teddy wrote to the Kennedys.

They included this year's family Christmas photo. "Merry Christmas & Happy New Year wishes with love from Turville".

Sitting front row centre were Teddy and Oliver with Uncle Colin and Aunt Eustacia standing behind them in the garden, Granny Crichton sitting in an armchair to their left. In the wingback chair to their right, their beloved Grandfather Crump, very soon to be Great-Grandfather Crump.

AND THEY LIVED HAPPILY EVER AFTER.

5. Caroline's Waterloo: My Take on Her Fake

The Betty Neels fan site published a hilarious summary of Caroline's Waterloo of Caroline's Waterloo, which I consider TBG at her golden age apogee. Quite a few readers do not agree, citing several events in the book. You know what I mean – the most egregious being his nasty comment on naming the beaten, pregnant jenny donkey Caroline rescues from the tinkers and her infamous fake runaway. In the next few posts, I will share my reflections on a select number of these.

First up, her fake runaway. Some readers had thought her letter to Radinck informing him she was leaving him (and then not carrying out that threat) was beneath the intrepid Caroline. It was thought she was behaving recklessly putting him through several hours of misery as he sought her out in the usual places, only to resignedly come home – to find calming knitting in their stately home, Huis Thoe.

They also think it was unfair of her to invoke this sort of nuclear option, to get him to talk. But then I looked at the context of her actions. As stated in the book, Caroline gave her plan a great deal of thought and carefully crafted her letter. What provoked her actions were his own fake statements. (You may be a baron, but you can act like a goof, Radinck!)

The previous evening, Radinck had informed his wife he was going away for several days. He openly tested Caroline's resolve to stick to the original MOC terms – and sighed that she was holding firm to that.

After their morning contretemps (more on his part than hers), Caroline merely picked up the phone and put on her Nancy Drew hat. She cleverly checked out his story with his administrative staff. Professor Baron Radinck Thoe van Ercklens had a full schedule and there were no travel plans at all. And certainly not to Dordrecht.

Ah, yes, Dordrecht. His first and most hamhanded attempt to test the waters with Caroline involved two whoppers: letting Caroline believe he was attracted to the young Dutch woman in the car crash by driving her all the way home south from Friesland to Dordrecht. And also intimating he stayed over at her house.

Talk about clueless! Did he think the green-eyed monster would phase Caroline? A one-woman donkey-rescuing virago? Sometimes overlooked is how she came to the aid of the pregnant donkey. It was a breezy grey day in Friesland when she came across the tinker family who took turns abusing the pregnant donkey. Fearlessly Caroline grabbed the whip off some snarky teenage tinker and threw it into the canal! So she was outnumbered and had limited Dutch, Caroline was righting an injustice! The donkey was not even hers, but Caroline untied the pregnant jenny and was making off with someone else's property. The shy Caroline asserted herself as the Baroness Thoe and pointed out her home and decided to adopt the donkey regardless of what anyone – tinker, tailor, Baron, Noakes – had to say about it.

Professor Baron, did you really think that the jenny-rescuing Caroline would take your proported infatuation with Miss

97

Dordrecht at face value? Jealousy would not prevent her from checking out the situation for herself.

If anything, it was not Caroline who was stooping low with a fake, it was Radinck. After all, it was just a decade ago that he was the victim of partner infidelity. His first wife took off with another man! It affected him so profoundly that Radinck shut off his heart and became a hermit. So this attempt to make Caroline jealous with a younger, prettier woman was pretty low…

Caroline showed through her letter what her limits were. Sheet anchor, yes. Mari complaisant of the female persuasion -> No Way. She would pack her bags and take her delightful sheet anchor self off the premises. It also serves notice that even the hint of another woman is unacceptable to her. If he had something to say and if he wanted her to stay, Radinck had better not hide behind 'silky tone of voice' and snubs and neglect – her reaction to his juvenile tactics had elicited the response from Baroness Caroline of raising the bar for him even higher!

You go, girl!

NEXT: Not a fake, part 2

Part 2. The Mystery of the Lady's Handkerchief. ..

Readers often think the handkerchief is an undotted 'i' in Caroline's Waterloo… What is the scrap of cloth that he 'carries like a lovesick boy'? Perhaps the proud Professor Baron Radinck Thoe van Ercklens sneaks into her room and snoops in her cupboard… With the interconnectedness of his and her bathrooms, dressing rooms, and bedrooms, that is possible. Faintly possible. Another option is we can decipher the clues in Chapter 4.

This is a new handkerchief of Caroline's, unused, so she fails to recognize it in the wee hours after they help Queenie in her foaling in Chapter 6. In paragraph 5 of the extraordinarily long and eventful chapter 4, we read that Sister Pringle of Oliver's gifted her with a set of handkerchiefs. This is the same supervisor who was engaged, about to get married, and was to leave her job 'make way for you' careerwise. What they about best-laid plans… Turns out Caroline ended up steaking a march and getting married first…

TGB emphasizes continually so far in the book the paucity of Caroline's worldly posessions, she made her own rug, borrowed books from the library, and had little more to her name besides her clothes, kitchenware, and dear Waterloo the cat. And then by contrast after her final day of work, TGB goes into some detail of what Caroline has strewn around the divan of her modest bedsit on Meadow Road… The handkerchiefs were part of a what she was unexpectedly 'burdened with" – farewell/wedding presents from patients and fellow nurses from Oliver's on her last day.

"She would have liked some new luggage to pack them in, but her case, although shabby, was quite adequate and she wanted a few pounds in her purse". TGB takes pains to emphasize that Caroline did not have the luxury of purchasing extra Samsonite to pack these gifts. Handkerchiefs are easy to squeeze into her case but a tea set from the other 3 members of the bicycling quarted and a cut-glass vase and a pink towel…! It seems that Caroline probably found a cardboard box or bags from the grocery store for these extra items.

Radinck pays Caroline a surprise visit shortly afterwards while she is sitting on the aforementioned rug toasting bread for her tea. He remarks on the presents on her divan. From this exchange, he is mentally calculating how to manage the transportation of her case, plus the soon-to-be packed presents, and Waterloo. It would not be done quickly, especially the fragility of the vase and tea set, so he concludes in his mind that packing the car before the wedding could make them late for the church ceremony. Because when you think of it, that must be the reason they drove to Meadow Road.

Radick picked her up, headed to the church, they quickly got married, then double backed to her bedsit 'Caro's luggage was put in the boot' , and then they headed to the ferry.

Upon arrival at Huis Thoe, the newly-weds were welcomed immediately into the drawing room where the entire staff had a surprise cake. To avoid hurting anyone's feelings, Caroline thanked the staff, which prompted Radinck to play along, asking for 6 bottles of champagne for the celebration… He was anxious to get back to his solitude and this further delayed his time in his study. With a head full of steam, you can picture the Baron afterwards going to the car with Noakes and male staff, peremptorily unloading first the case from the boot. Then seeing a box or bag or two fallen on its side, he hurriedly but courteously passed them over to Jan or young Willem. Slamming the lid, giving the keys to Noakes and closetting himself with his notes and books and papers…

Next day, leaving the huis early without giving Caroline a chance to see him, the Baron grumpily drives to the hospital. Radick goes to the boot for his medical bag… and spots a stray handkerchief messing up its pristine, sporty interior. Moodily he jams this into his coat pocket (it is a cool early November) with the intention of handing it over to Caroline…

As the days passed, Radinck unconsciously kept refusing to return her handkerchief, so this scrap of cloth became… something more. Can you picture him driving more than 2 hours south from Huis Thoe with the decorative young Juffrouw van Doorn through the snow to Dordrecht, (near Belgium, which might as well be France, and we know that entire country is full of Brighton!). For his protection, he absentmindedly fingering this cloth, this talisman of his wife. A reassuring embodiment of the later conscious surrendering of his solitude, Professor Baron Thoe van Ercklens wryly knows he has become another of the spoils of war.. the biggest prize of Caroline's Waterloo.

6. Heaven is Gentle (and Christian won't go down without a fight)

Updating Heaven is Gentle by Betty Neels…

Attempt #1 to leave Eliza: Christian tells Eliza candidly after breakfast that he is attracted to her because she is very pretty, kind, energetic, feminine, brings out his protective instincts… but this all interferes with the way he has planned his life – work, a wife who doesn't disturb the smooth flow of his days… and since we not meet again after today, Good-bye!

a swoop, and "I'll never forget you," a ferocious kiss, and then he opens the door, pushes her into the foyer, and closes the door on her, EVERMORE.

Then, less than TWELVE hours later, Christian has to call her back because his friend Professor William Wyllie has a heart/asthma something…

Attempt #2 to get away from The Great Disturbance in The Force AKA Exquisite Eliza Proudfoot. …

This time, the following day, Christian decides to *ahem* sneak away from Professor Wyllie's without saying good-bye. And taking the easy way out by having his FFR Hub write a farewell note. (Hub shakes his head privately…)

"Ja, mission accomplished. " thinks Christian as the plane heads to Schipol, "Eliza is now part of the past…"
(Ha! Did the wee man really think he would get away so easily? Cupid (in the form of Professor Wyllie) and his accomplice Dr Trent are hatching up something over the next couple weeks…)

Attempt #3. Travel to Dorset to consult on a patient at the request of a colleague, Sir Harry Bliss, and drop in on Eliza's parents in Charmouth, Dorset.

(Why did Wylie& Trent insist on having HER accompany the Prof to Huis van Duyl?)

Christian wanted to confirm 'only terrible people could result in a slip of a girl with the temerity to Make Me Sweep With a Broom.'

Attempt #4. Reminded his MOM to butt out of his love life.

"…do not allow yourself to forget that Estelle and I plan to marry within the next few months."

Crack open TWO bottles of champagne to celebrate doing so with such finesse…

Attempt #5. Talk incessantly about how much he wants to marry his fiancée Estelle

Christian prattles on about Estelle's deftness as a hostess to EVERYONE in the library, resulting in Prof Wyllie's nasty attack… (a la Mijnheer Kok wheezing at the sight or mere thought of his mother-in-law… coincidence?)

And brag about the size of the rock he slipped on Estelle's finger (Eliza's eyes glazed over…)

Attempt #6. Treat Eliza exactly like Doctor Berrevoets and any other house guest… A formal note for a walk before breakfast, pleasant enquiries as to Eliza's plans upon leaving Huis van Duyl, talk about the intricacies of meteorological forecasting, offer all his guests the incredible treat of Dinner & Dancing @ The Rijn Hotel.

#7. She will never have lunch in This Town again…!
Righteous indignation at Eliza for messing up the numbers at The Rijn…! 3 men – Christian, Dr Peters, Professor Wylie. And with Eliza offering some lame excuse about writing letters, only 2 women – Mom and Estelle…! What will the maitre d' @ The Rijn think?

"I am shocked at Eliza, Shocked…"

#8… inside the mind of Prof Christian van Duyl:

"Heres the plan: Look for Estelle to talk because Wyllie says he observed MY fiancee kissing Dr john Peters. Such nonsense… but sensible to have a word. Mom and Professor Wylie say Estelle is having an afternoon strolling near the trees by the lake… off to see her there…

Forgot my gloves in the small sitting room… went back and overheard MOM and WYLLIE smugly congratulating themselves for arranging to get a new man for Estelle and a new woman for me. Sir Harry was in this too, apparently! And Trent! "We should have tried for a male nurse… No time to interview her…" Ha!

And Wylie unapologetically admitted to his deceit, "Of course, boy. You were so fixed on marrying for all sorts of puerile ideas. Wouldn't listen to a single soul with brains. Now this little lass is whom you should marry. Shake up your life... That skinny one, ha! Not a moment of happiness... Mark my words."

Going to the lake now to suggest to Estelle that we set a date for the wedding to stop these plots... As I depart, I suavely leave this band of conspirators with, "Did you also arrange for the CAT as well...?"

#9. Finale: Epilogue. Christian van Duyl waves the white flag:

"That's low, Mom, I didn't stand a chance when I overheard John Peters and Estelle talking... and then the angel, Eliza, emerging from the trees with Her Hair Down... and I can only say, 'Mom, you are right, I give in. Are you happy now?'

Whaat, you want how many grandchildren?

I will certainly do my best...!"

"And as for you, Wylie, I do thank you."Christian adds silkily, "they say one good deed deserves another. Sir, I alert you that your bachelor days are henceforth numbered."

Wylie chokes, and Christian cheerfully obliges by thumping the professor's back.

AND THEY LIVED HAPPILY EVER AFTER

ABOUT THE AUTHOR

MeiMei Long writes to delight herself and she hopes readers enjoys spending time with her stories. She has updated several of the best novels of Betty Neels. A true fan, MeiMei keeps to the spirit of the original books but brings a bit of 21st century nuances to the Happily Ever Afters.

As far as she is concerned, MeiMei Long knows the world of Betty Neels women and men still exist! You just need to hang around good people who share her appreciation of people acting like Ladies and Gentlemen - and find them!)

www.ingramcontent.com/pod-product-compliance
Lightning Source LLC
Chambersburg PA
CBHW070457130626
46555CB00003B/1039